Henry's war is a private one — with himself. He is a personal pacifist, with no desire to convert others, but only to be left to lead his life in his own way. We meet him first contentedly churning out moderately successful and highly unlikely spy stories in his Chelsea flat, and engaged, almost by accident, to Veronica, a high-brow militant Aldermaston marcher. When Britain resorts to 'gunboat' tactics in the Castillian Islands, his private idyll is rudely shattered. He breaks with his overbearing fiancée and flees to a hill-farm in Wales to avoid his call-up. But he finds it is not so easy to escape from the corporate demands of the society he lives in, nor from the implications of his own nature when suddenly faced by the warm-hearted Albertine, whose talent for love and need for protection make their special demands on him.

3/6 £1.25

HENRY'S WAR

BY

JEREMY BROOKS

LONDON

MACMILLAN & CO LTD

NEW YORK · ST MARTIN'S PRESS

1962

MACMILLAN AND COMPANY LIMITED
St. Martin's Street London WC2
also Bombay Calcutta Madras Melbourne

THE MACMILLAN COMPANY OF CANADA LIMITED
Toronto

ST MARTIN'S PRESS INC
New York

PRINTED IN GREAT BRITAIN

For
The Landlord and Customers
The Brondanw Arms,
Llanfrothen

5. The proud have hid a snare for me, and cords; they have spread a net by the wayside; they have set gins for me. Selah.

PSALM 140

STITCH-IN-TIME DEPT.

If the 'Castillian Emergency', vaguely suggested here, bears any resemblance to any other emergency, living or dead, that is only because history is tediously repetitive in its patterns. If current regulations affecting the Army conflict with anything in this book, I don't care.

Chapter One

A MOTH had somehow gained entrance to Henry's mosquito net. Henry lay on his back and watched with resentment as it gyrated clumsily about the apex of his little muslin tent. What was the use of a mosquito net, he grumbled to himself, if even a moth could get into it? They were much bigger than mosquitoes. Then it occurred to him that the moth had quite possibly lain dormant in the bed before the net had been erected; or might even have been born there while he lay asleep. This solution satisfied Henry, and he became more cheerful.

Outside the window of Henry's bed-sitting-room a number of large damp snowflakes were sliding erratically down into Gloucester Road. Henry had seen them, in the grey hours of dawn, while he was being sick in the bathroom. Then the flakes had been even larger, but drier, ragged at the edges like pieces of old lace. Resting, pale but composed, on the rim of the handbasin, Henry had watched their slow descent into the brick canyon between the houses with quiet satisfaction. It was the first week of June, a time of year when one has a right to expect some firm manifestation of summer, not the last desperate gesture of winter. Such meteorological freaks invariably gave Henry a childish pleasure: that'll show 'em, he thought obscurely. But it had been cold in the bathroom, and he had returned, as soon as he felt some confidence in his stomach, to the warm safety of his mosquito net, feeling curiously spiritual now that the violence of the nausea had spent itself.

Waking now, some hours later, Henry's appreciation of the unseasonable weather outside was clouded by his determination to believe that he was in Aden, in the middle of July. 'The arid sun,' he muttered experimentally, 'shrivels a man's mind into a small, hard, emotionless pea.' No, bean. You can't have an emotionless pea.

Henry giggled, and shifted onto his side, pulling the netting aside so that he could see out into the room. Screwing up his eyes he saw, or told himself that he saw, the little splashes of dried blood spattered across the wall near his desk, where, the night before, he had been absent-mindedly massacring mosquitoes while working on the secret report for Brigadier McNeil. His own blood, he reminded himself. All over the Middle East, he reflected, in Cairo, Damascus, Beirut, Tel Aviv, Teheran, as far east as Kasrkand on the borders of Baluchistan, there were rooms like this where the walls carried these tiny legacies of his tough, indestructible body. Then there was the little pool of blood that had seeped into the earthen floor of his Caucasian prison, after he had been brought back from the 'interrogation' at which he had refused to reveal Domenica's hiding place; the toe he had had to hack off himself, with a piece of broken glass, during their escape down the Caspian Sea; the little finger that had been neatly amputated by a sniper's bullet as he escaped across the Embassy wall in Baghdad.

'Little bits of my body,' Henry murmured softly to himself, with emotion, 'scattered across half the world!'

Henry tossed restlessly under his mosquito net, seeming to feel the sweat spurt from his pores, soaking the single sheet that covered his nakedness. He reached under his pillow for his potato-gun, fondling the cold metal against his chest: a wicked little killer that would take the heart out of an ace at twenty yards. Henry's head ached, and his mouth was dry, sour-tasting; but he put from his mind the idea that this was the natural result of the ridiculous, unwanted pub-crawl of the night before, and instead fell to cursing, in the clipped understatements of a man to whom duty is a strict but well-loved mistress, the events which had condemned him to swelter dangerously in Aden at just the worst time of the year. He could still feel the sand under his fingernails from his ordeal in the desert, and in his nostrils the insidious red dust of the Yemen clogged and dried at every breath.

On Henry's bedside table there stood a half tumbler of clear brown liquid; beside it, a single egg. Henry reached an arm under the mosquito net, deftly, one-handedly, broke and emptied the egg into the tumbler, and drew the mixture into the secret world below the net. Leaning up on one elbow, he raised the glass to his lips, tossed the entire contents into his mouth, and, with some difficulty, swallowed. It was not a very pleasant experience. The cold tea had been rather stale, and eggs purchased in Kensington are seldom as fresh as one could wish. But lacking brandy, it was as near as Henry could get to a Hero's breakfast. 'There's nothing,' he said to himself firmly, 'like a Bombay Oyster for putting lead in the pencil.' No, that wouldn't do. 'For setting a man up'? It wouldn't do to start getting fussy about style at this stage. He wasn't supposed to be writing masterpieces, was he?

As if unjustly accused of an artistic crime, Henry got out of bed truculently, and for a moment stood shivering in the bleak London air. He looked long-ingly back at the mosquito net, that womb surrogate to which he had now become so attached that he could no longer write thrillers which were not set in a tropical climate for fear of losing his slender title to the thing; and regretfully decided that since it was now past noon, his day ought, in all conscience, to commence.

Henry was a man of habit, but he was not ruled by the clock. He liked to do his writing in the 'morning', but for his purposes the word indicated a period of time, probably about three and a half to four hours, between breakfast (usually orange juice — this morn-ing's Bombay Oyster had been a rare refinement) and lunch, a meal which in Henry's life not seldom occurred at five o'clock in the afternoon. During this period Henry would smoke about sixteen cigarettes, drink five or six cups of Instant coffee, and consume anything up to a quarter of a pound of Dolly Mixture. In moments of intense artistic travail he would play meaningless tunes on a bulbous little instrument called an ocarina, and when a mental blockage, or sheer boredom, brought work to a standstill he would stand with his back against the wall on one side of the room

and throw darts at the dartboard attached to the
opposite wall, a distance of exactly 8′ 6″. The wall
near the dartboard was pitted like a battlefield from
the days when Henry had first installed the game, but
now, after five and a half books written in the same
room, Henry rarely missed.

On this June morning, which was afternoon to the
rest of Europe, Henry spent much of the time at the
dartboard, none at all at the ocarina. He had started
well, still under the suggestive influence of the mosquito
net and the Bombay Oyster; but there was something,
quite distinct from the hangover and its attendant
remorse, nagging away at the back of his mind, refusing to come forward and identify itself yet by its in-
sistent nudging preventing him from losing himself
completely in the predicament of his hero. He would
dearly have liked a drink, but the Rules would not
allow him to leave his room until he had done 'a day's
work'. Henry thought of himself as a weak character,
and had therefore devised certain Rules intended to
reinforce the apparently boneless body of his life. He
was also possessed, intermittently, of a guilty conscience. This was due to what seemed his fortuitous
ability to earn an adequate income (adequate for him,
that is: about £10 a week) by working an average of
five and a half hours a day. If it had occurred to Henry,
which it didn't, that he worked a seven-day week and
had never had more than a week's holiday since he
became self-supporting, he would still have felt guilty.
It was astonishing, even bewildering, that he, among
so many millions and without the benefit of a private
income, a decent education, or even a recognisable

talent, should have broken free from that oppressive, mad, bad ogre, the employer. If necessary Henry would have worked ten hours a day, fourteen hours, just to stay free to choose which hours to work, and where to work, and when to eat, and what time to get up in the morning, and what clothes to wear.

This morning, as was usual after a beery evening, Henry found himself in a mood of cool detachment when facing his work. The magic which had been so abundantly present in the words when, during the previous day's creative afflatus, they had come tumbling forth, had now flown, leaving only the known pattern of the advancing plot to reassure him that each line was not, in fact, totally meaningless. To establish even this bridgehead on the shores of despair was in itself an act of faith. Looking back over the work of the last few weeks Henry could find little in it to commend. It would get by, that was about all. But there was no liveliness, no spontaneity — and Henry knew why: Veronica. Ah, well.

At such times as this, with that whatever-it-was scratching away just below his consciousness and an all-too-clear apprehension of the way his work was slipping, the only thing to do was to search for mechanical flaws. Henry was fortunate in lighting upon a major mistake almost immediately. It appeared that in the heat of the moment his hero, Peter Colchester (the nom-de-guerre, it was sometimes hinted, of the younger son of a marquess), had absent-mindedly left his devoted Chinese servant, Wu Pin Chi, in the hands of that Russian-controlled band of disaffected Arabs from whom Colchester himself had only recently escaped. This would not do at all. It was not the act of a gentleman, and, besides, Wu Pin Chi would be needed for the next book. Since it was not possible, with only 15,000 words to go, to send Colchester off on a daring and dangerous rescue mission, the only thing to be done was to go back and cut out all reference to the Chinaman in the pages leading up to Colchester's capture. This would have the advantage of freeing another 2,000 or so words, and it was always convenient to have a small margin in hand when winding up a book.

This task occupied Henry for more than an hour. He then retyped those pages which had suffered the worst mutilation, carefully knitting the ragged ends of paragraphs together with an absolute minimum of fresh composition. This accomplished, Henry began to feel happier. His 'morning' was wearing on; things — if only negative things — were being achieved; guilt was being waved back like a woman of the streets into its dark doorway. Henry put the kettle on and started to play himself round the board: a double to start, treble one, double four, double nine, nineteen, twenty, the starting double, the bull — eight darts.

But even his darts playing was not up to standard today. He missed the double nine, had to go for double ten, got a single, was tempted to pretend that it had been a double, and gave up in disgust.

When you start cheating against yourself it's time to take a long cold look at your opponent. The previous evening's drinking had been unusually heavy: had been, Henry emended honestly, stupidly excessive. There is no pleasure in drinking like that, in getting so drunk that you couldn't even remember, next morning, how the evening had ended. And with this thought there floated to the surface of Henry's mind the memory which, submerged but active, had lain unrecognised between himself and his work ever since he woke up. Something had happened last night. He had met someone. A girl. He had done something dreadful, been rude, been insufferable in some way. Was that all? The emotion of shame was strong there, without the cause. What had he done, what was the girl's name? He would certainly get nothing useful done until he had found out.

It was a relief when the telephone rang. Henry's hatred and love of this instrument see-sawed daily, but even when he was loathing it most bitterly he would admit that at times its sudden shattering ring called out in tones of nothing less than salvation, as now.

'Veronica!' he said warmly. 'You've no idea how glad I am to hear your voice. This damned room's absolutely chock full of nothing this morning.'

'You've been drinking again,' said Veronica, without sympathy. 'Anyway, it's afternoon, not morning. I suppose you haven't even had lunch yet?'

'Not yet, no.'

'You know it's nearly six o'clock, I suppose? When did you last eat?'

'I had an egg for breakfast.' Henry had been tempted to say that he had had a Bombay Oyster for breakfast, but Veronica never would understand about his relationship with Peter Colchester.

'That's not much for a whole day's fuel intake. Are you working?'

'Sort of.'

'That means you're not. Have you got a hangover?'

'A bit.'

Veronica's voice softened. She hated Henry to go drinking, but he knew it was one of his attractions for her; it gave her reforming zeal something solid to bite on. Henry had even, at times, caught himself pretending to be a drunkard, which he wasn't, in order to heighten her interest in him.

'Oh, Henry, dear, why do you do it? Are you unhappy? Lonely? Is the book going badly again? Where did you go last night? Whom were you with?'

Nobody he had ever met, Henry thought, could bring out a 'whom' with such assurance.

'Well, no-one really . . .'

'You weren't drinking alone?'

'No, no, I met some people . . .'

'What people?'

'I can't remember. Oh, there was this Irishman in Mooney's, but he started picking a quarrel so I left. Then there were some other people somewhere else . . .'

'And you can't even remember who they were?'

'Not very clearly, no.'

'Oh, *Henry!*'

Henry might have felt some resentment at this inquisition (though it was fairly usual) had he not been trying so hard, for reasons of his own, to remember whom in fact he had been with the previous night. He was almost grateful to Veronica for forcing him to make the effort, for he had indeed uncovered one vital clue. The incident with the girl, whatever it had been, had taken place in Cheyne Walk. The pub they had issued from had been near there, which considerably narrowed the field of search. Henry was already dimly aware that there would have to be a search.

'As a matter of fact,' he said mildly, 'I would rather like to remember who they were. One of them was rather nice.'

'I wish you wouldn't do it, dear,' said Veronica, a little more tartly. 'There's absolutely no need, you've got lots of friends, and you can always come here if you're feeling a bit lonely, there's always *somebody* at home . . .'

Yes, thought Henry, always somebody: poor Aunt Ada, deaf as a post, Aunt Bea, smelling of dogs, and Mrs. Timberley, waving pieces of gauze and smiling wanly, bravely, from her imaginary sick-bed. Always somebody to listen to on embroidery, kennel discipline, and extra-sensory perception.

'. . . and you know you can have a drink here if you want one.'

'Sherry,' said Henry.

'What's wrong with sherry?'

'I prefer beer.'

'Well,' said Veronica briskly, changing the subject, 'you'll have to put up with sherry tonight because there's no beer and I want you to come round about seven — no, don't say "but, but, but" like that, this is important — I want you to come and meet some people and help us think of something to do about this dreadful Castillian business. It's no good everyone just being shocked by it, someone's got to *do* something. And you must help, Henry. I know you will.'

'What Castillian business?'

'I mean the — *Henry!* Henry, you can't tell me you don't even *know* what's been happening in the Castillian Islands?'

'Not the faintest, I'm afraid,' said Henry cheerfully. 'I say, are you going to feed me tonight?'

'Yes, of course. Honestly, Henry, you are hopeless. Don't you read the newspapers at all?'

'Only the bits about sex, on Sundays.' Henry had long ago given up reading newspapers. He very easily became upset by the cruelty and dishonesty he saw on every hand if he raised his head to take a quick look at the world. He had his living to earn, after all; it was impossible to concentrate on the remarkable adventures of Peter Colchester when one was sweating with fear and anger at the extraordinary follies being perpetrated all over the world. Better to keep one's head down and hope that the megalomaniacs in power would allow one to remain alive a little longer. Henry had never been able to understand how it was that people like Veronica could daily remind themselves of all the terrible things that were happening everywhere — starvation, disease, massacre, persecution, oppression — and still go on trotting sociably around, doing little or nothing about it: a balance of mind as impossible to conceive, for Henry, as that of Christians who go gaily to war, or devote their lives to amassing riches.

This Castillian business, however, whatever it might be, had certainly got Veronica excited. Henry didn't understand a word she was saying (indeed, he was not clear whether these islands were in the West Indies or the East Indies) but the word 'perfidy' came across clearly, and it was soon obvious that whatever was happening Veronica strongly disapproved of her own country's part in it.

'I can't take all that in over the phone,' said Henry, 'you'll have to explain when you see me. About seven, was it?'

'Seven, and sober.'

'You've never seen me drunk.'

'Well, I don't want to start now. Do you love me?'

'Er — yes,' said Henry.

The kettle had nearly boiled dry and the room was full of steam. It was still only just after six. If he hurried he would have time for a quick and comforting pint before he faced a roomful of Veronica's intimidating friends. He sat down at his desk, crossed out a word, substituted another, and then rubbed out both and put back the original word. He wrote neat numbers into the corners of the two pages he had written soon after leaving his bed, counted up the number of words he had saved by cutting out the Wu Pin Chi incidents, and wrote the figure '58,500' at the foot of a column of similar figures on his scribbling pad. He then rose from his desk, his working day complete.

He dressed quickly for the street. A sober Cheviot tweed suit, brown Harris overcoat, dark brown shoes without toe-caps, woollen gloves (because he lost them too often to afford leather ones) and a green felt hat of variable shape. His tie was of knitted wool, as worn, he believed, by Wykehamists, his cream shirt newly laundered. Henry always dressed neatly when going to visit Veronica, and always experienced the

same twinge of guilt at what he felt to be the deception
he was thus engaging in. Disguised as a junior university lecturer, he was the slave of evil impulses: to
take taxis, tip porters, march boldly up to policemen
with spurious enquiries simply in order to be addressed
as 'Sir'.

He went into the bathroom, opened the little cup-
board above the handbasin, and extracted a roll of
pound notes from a toothpaste packet. He put three
of the notes in his wallet and replaced the roll in its
hiding place. He suffered from an unnatural fear of
burglars which, notwithstanding the potato-gun under
his pillow, had increased considerably since he had
been writing the Peter Colchester books: Krossov,
Colchester's enemy, could penetrate the stoutest defences with nothing stronger than a kirby-grip.

In the sitting-room Henry opened the window a
fraction to let the steam out, and jammed an ebony
ruler under the frame to prevent it from being opened
from the outside. In his overcoat pocket he put the
notebook which he had long since ceased to use but
which from habit and a constitutional desire to be
prepared for anything he still carried. Thus equipped,
with the door locked in two places, and the keys in his
pocket, Henry set off, without enthusiasm, to take
dinner with the girl to whom he had somehow become
engaged.

Chapter Two

Henry's engagement to Veronica was more of a mystery to his friends than it was to hers. Veronica moved in circles in which other people's actions tended to be judged rather than analysed. If they had permitted themselves to think about it they would have conceded that, although it could not be considered a 'good match' in social terms, it was at least a liaison consistent with Veronica's character, for she was a girl who had early shown signs of having inherited the Timberley leaning towards Good Works. Happily a Welsh accent, far from being embarrassing, was actually rather charming; and although it was said that these books of his (which no-one had actually read) were the sort of things one sees on railway book-stalls in garish paper covers, at least his occupation allowed one to hope that Veronica might lead him towards higher things. Didn't Balzac write romances until he was over thirty? And anyway, it made it possible to introduce him as 'a writer'. He didn't seem very interested in the spiritual side of life, but no doubt Veronica would alter that; and he had himself admitted to having pacifist leanings, which was a very good sign. On the whole it was thought that Veronica, who could be relied upon to land herself with a problem husband, had made a very fair compromise: certainly a relief after all those Indians and Africans she used to bring home from the Church Social Research Centre.

Henry's friends had had less opportunity of weighing up his future wife. Veronica would not accompany him to the pubs which were the linked centres of his social life, and none of his friends was the sort of person who would have thanked him for an invitation to take sherry with Mrs. Timberley, poor Aunt Ada, Aunt Bea and Veronica in Eaton Mews South. Those that had met her had done so accidentally in Henry's bed-sitting-room: occasions which left Henry in a state of schizophrenic frenzy, for he could no more adopt in front of Veronica the persona which he was accustomed to present to his pubby friends than he could allow one of them to observe him in his role as a neophyte Timberley.

If, on one of these occasions, Veronica was the first to leave, the friend's reaction was likely to be: 'Well, well, I'd never have believed it! They said you'd dug up a fossil, old boy, but, man, they didn't say how deep you'd been digging! I didn't know there were any of that sort left.' But it was not within their code to criticise, or commend in any other way. Veronica was, after all, female, and not unattractive; if she was what Henry wanted, well — every man to his own perversion. In their world one was permitted any peculiarity in one's private life so long as it didn't obtrude on one's public-house life; and the brighter ones, particularly the females, may even have acknowledged to themselves that liaisons and marriages formed from within the drinking group seldom lasted for long. Some men lived with their mothers; some had dull wives at home, or jolly wives who came out drinking with them; some lived in near-slums, others in luxury service flats; some were architects and doctors and solicitors, others were stage-hands, printers, barrow-boys. As for many people, beer was not the main attraction of pub life: it was the social anonymity, the instinctive recognition by pub-goers that a man leads many lives simultaneously, and that they are often not compatible with each other.

If, on the other hand, the friend were to leave before Veronica, she would either say: 'What a fascinating man, darling! Honestly, I can't understand the way you always refuse to bring your friends along to the Mews, as if you were ashamed of them, or something! I think you're a bit of a snob, on the quiet.' Or: 'Really, Henry, you do pick up some extraordinary creatures! What *can* you have in common with a scruffy little man like that? I know how good-hearted you are, darling, but I really don't think you ought to let him *sleep* here — that type always makes trouble in the end, you know.'

The one person who fully understood how Henry had come to get engaged to Veronica was Charlie Evans, Henry's oldest and dearest friend. Henry seldom saw Charlie these days. Veronica had fought their friendship bitterly, with every weapon in her armoury, perhaps sensing how dangerous to her such male love could be; but this alone would not have influenced Henry. But Charlie had, since arriving in London, become a Catholic; and this, combined with the fact that he now worked, for a pittance, in an

16

East End boys' club and could seldom be persuaded
to come 'up West', had somehow, despite their mutual
efforts, driven a wedge between them. Charlie made
no attempt to convert Henry; Henry never questioned
his friend's change of faith. But an area of experience
had been wired off, warning notices had gone up, and
many of the common footpaths between two minds
had fallen into disuse. Henry still thought of Charlie
as his 'best friend', but only in a crisis, now, would
he seek him out.

Charlie and Henry had known each other ever since
they were old enough to go to the primary school at
Bont Newydd. They had been through the forms at
Blaengwyrionedd Grammar School side by side; and
at seventeen, mutually and in each case mistakenly
deciding that the peacetime army offered a good career
to bright boys, they had signed on together for a five-
year engagement. For many of those years they had
served together, Charlie even deliberately losing his
third stripe when he realised that Henry was never
going to be offered one; and when their time was up,
and Charlie announced that he intended to settle in
London and get himself trained as a social worker, it
never even occurred to Henry that he might stay on
in Wales.

Charlie, as the son of a Minister, naturally made
straight for the Y.M.C.A. when they arrived in London. Henry, as irreligious as he was unmilitary,
followed. They stayed there for less than a week; but
it was through this, for Henry, unlikely medium that
he met Veronica.

Henry had never met, seen or heard of anyone like

Veronica in his life before. In his experience women were either the sultry, desirable creatures of his mosquito-net imaginings (in which class were included, although they never approached the ideal, both the shopgirls and typists of his early flirtations and the amateur and professional whores of his army adventures), or married, dull, and wholly undesirable. He would have acknowledged that there was a third class: the smart, sophisticated, long-legged beauties of the advertisements and the social gossip columns — but he conceived of them as being a purely fictional, certainly never-to-be-encountered variation.

But Veronica was different. She dressed well; had a reasonably attractive face and body; never giggled suggestively or picked up a *double-entendre*; would talk for hours on subjects other than sex without appearing in the least bored; and, above all, held unconventional opinions without a trace of shame. This last was important to Henry, who had been so often bewildered at finding himself in a minority over issues in which the truth seemed to him self-evident. Having no training in nor aptitude for abstract thought, he was easily overwhelmed in argument; and had come to look upon himself as some sort of freak.

Veronica changed all this; not because he often found himself in agreement with her, but because, by encouraging him to think better of himself, she helped him towards a sense of his own identity. Of course he very quickly discovered that her opinions were not unconventional at all, but merely conformed to a convention which Henry had not come across before. But by this time the good work was done. And by this time, too, while Henry was still in the flush of discovering this exciting other world to which Veronica belonged, they had, on Veronica's initiative, become engaged.

Charlie had watched this process silently but with apprehension. He could have predicted with some accuracy, two years ago, the stage in his relationship with Veronica and the whole Timberley set-up that Henry had now reached. But it would have done no good. For even if he had spoken of it now, with Henry already dimly aware that all was not well between himself and his fiancée, Henry would not have known what he was talking about.

Chapter Three

'I WISH you could have met my mother,' said Captain Herbert. 'A wonderful woman, truly wonderful. I don't suppose the world will see her like again. Does that sound excessive? I'm sorry. Veronica reminds me of her not a little at times, do you know. A dear girl. You are a very fortunate young man. My uncle, the Brigadier, who as you know was Veronica's god-father, used to remark on the resemblance when she was quite a small girl . . . although of course there is no relationship whatsoever . . . unless perhaps through my Marloe cousins? . . . in any case very distant. I don't think you knew my uncle?'

'I didn't, I'm afraid,' said Henry.

'A remarkable man. I'm sorry, dear boy, is that your sherry? A man of quite extraordinary insight! I well remember his predicting, while I was still at Sandhurst, that I would never marry. And do you know, *I never have!* Isn't that remarkable?'

'Remarkable,' said Henry.

Captain Herbert was himself no ordinary figure. He was a small, sandy man, his face pinched by a multiplicity of conflicting lines into an expression of sad sweetness, enhanced rather than disguised by a fierce ginger moustache. He wore a thick yellowish tweed suit; a pair of openwork sandals revealing small areas

20

of pale mauve sock; and a white polo-necked sweater, ribbed in enormous cable-stitch patterns, on the chest of which was sewn an embroidered circular badge declaring its wearer to be the winner of the Open Downhill Slalom, Sestriere, 1936. A gold-rimmed monocle on a thin chain swung elegantly across these expanses of dazzling whiteness, adding the final touch to an appearance which somehow contrived to convey both freedom from the standardised normalities of society and a respectful nostalgia for the trampled corpse of Edwardiana. It was perhaps the painful sweetness of Captain Herbert's smile that saved him from any suggestion of sportiness. 'A queer dear,' Veronica called him, despite Henry's awkward objections to the phrase. His appearances at Mrs. Timberley's dinner table were an unfathomable mystery.

'Our dear hostess,' said Captain Herbert, 'seems anxious to attract your attention. Am I to lose you, then? Do try to come back to me, dear boy. Neither of us, of course, are militarists now, but our army background does give us something in common, don't you think?'

Henry smiled encouragingly and, clutching his tiny glass of sherry, crossed the overfurnished room to where Veronica's mother, still trailing wisps of a pre-Raphaelite beauty, fluttered her hands from her station near the door. Despite her unfailingly apologetic air, Henry, standing before her, always felt that she might mete out some dreadful punishment if he were to displease her.

'Dear Henry, I did so want to have a little talk with you. Veronica will be here in a moment, she's just helping Nanny with the dinner.' Mrs. Timberley paused, as always, to give Henry an opportunity for the token kiss that was the conventional greeting in this family; but which, as always, Henry could not bring himself to give.

'You know, my dear, that this is rather a *special* little gathering? Just the ones we're really sure about — so few, so dreadfully few! Veronica has a little plot afoot — I'm sure you'll approve of it — and she did so want the support of one or two really *distinguished* people. Oh, the terrible, terrible things that happen in the world today!

'Do you know everyone here? No, of course you don't. I saw you talking to dear Captain Herbert, such a sweet man, why he never married I just can't imagine, he was such a pretty boy when he was young, too. And then, somehow, the wars never seemed to come at quite the right time for him. A really brilliant family. His brother, you know, Sir Caspar, got his "K" before he was forty — and then had to go and get eaten by cannibals or something, such a pity. We're really very lucky to have Captain Herbert with us, I always think converts are so useful, don't you? Ah, my dear, how I hate the thought of war! I'm convinced that it is only the courage of young men like you that will save the world in the end. You must be the world's conscience — ah, I can see you're smiling, but I know how deeply you feel this too!

'You know Mrs. Ordovice, of course, and poor Aunt Ada, and Aunt Bea. I don't think you've met Philip, he's a publisher, only children's books but a man of real principle. And that's Margaret Arcadia, over by the book-case, she's writing a thesis on something-or-other, no, no, not for an examination, this is for the Church Social Research Group, yes, Veronica's little affair. And over by the hearth, that's Mr. Winchester, whom you really must meet, a born orator . . . ah, here comes Veronica . . . Veronica, darling, Henry and I have been having a delightful cosy little chat over here in the corner before you start coming to bully us with all your problems . . . ah, that's what I like to see, a nice warm kiss, how wonderful to be young, and in love!'

It wasn't a very warm kiss, in fact, despite Henry's gratitude to Veronica for his deliverance from Mrs. Timberley. It would have taken more courage, or cruelty, than Henry had to have denied a kiss to the pale cheek which was offered by Veronica. But he was acutely aware that there had been a moment, just before he had bent his face dutifully towards hers, when his flesh had shrunk from that contact. It was absurd, of course: some momentary transfer from mother to daughter of that purely accidental revulsion . . . and yet: and yet, Henry was suddenly filled with panic. Such a thing ought not to be possible. His mind began whirling with a thousand doubts, and, as always in a crisis, his immediate instinct was to get away, to be by himself and let the revolving thoughts settle into their new pattern before being called upon to say or do anything at all. He knew at once that he could not now under any circumstances stay for dinner.

Veronica slipped her arm through his and led him towards an unoccupied corner of the room. She was

tall, straight and slim, with little pointed breasts which
Henry had once found rather fetching but which he
now perceived to have been borrowed from some
other, differently fashioned body. Why, he wondered
frantically, this sudden onset of unfair physical
criticism? He glanced covertly at her square, wide-
browed face, and admitted openly to himself for the
first time that her mouth was too small and that her
large brown eyes, on which he had often compli-
mented her, exophthalmically bulged. Such thoughts
were unwelcome, and Henry put them from him as
firmly as he knew how. This was not, however, a
form of self-discipline at which he was well-practised,
and throughout their conversation he continued to
search her face anxiously, eager to discover, and to
latch firmly on to, whatever it had been about her that
had once attracted him to the point of proposal — or
rather, to the point of accepting Veronica's proposal.

She seemed, now, unusually anxious to please him.
'I'm sorry you got caught by Mummy,' she said. 'I
know how you hate it, though I do think you're rather
silly about it, it's only that silly inferiority complex
of yours at work, after all. I had to help Nanny with
the grub, she's furious because we didn't tell her
about there being so many for dinner in time . . .'

'Well, I'm afraid I shan't be able . . .'

'And so of course she was right up the wall, and
poor Aunt Ada isn't in any state to help and of course
today of all days Mrs. B. didn't turn up so the washing
up isn't done from breakfast let alone the rest, so
heaven knows what we'll all eat and you're probably
starving too . . .'

'As a matter of fact I shan't . . .'

'. . . but you'll be able to sneak round the larder later if you're still hungry. Now, the thing is, about this Castillian business . . .' The Timberley habit of never listening to anything anyone said sometimes had its advantages; tonight Henry found it maddening. He was quite prepared to listen to whatever Veronica had to say about 'the Castillian business', but not to go on sipping sherry under false pretences. 'Veronica,' he said, 'listen, Veronica, I shan't be able to stay for dinner, so hadn't you better go and tell Nanny . . . ?'

'Not stay for . . . ? Now, don't be silly, dear, it's all fixed, now, anyway, I need you, I need your support, this is *important*, Henry!'

'I'm sorry. You know I'd love to stay, but I can't. When you rang this afternoon it quite slipped my mind that I'd promised to meet Charlie Evans tonight, and there's no way I could have got in touch to put him off. I shall have to go, I'm afraid.'

This was a clever lie. Henry had given, as his alibi, the one person in whom Veronica would immediately believe as her evening's rival, since he was, as it were, a forbidden friend. Thinking of Charlie Evans, and of his fictional appointment with him (where? — in 'The Onions', of course), Henry glanced anxiously at his watch, telling himself that if he allowed a quarter of an hour for getting down to Blackfriars Bridge, he had better not stay at Veronica's for more than another twenty minutes.

'I'm meeting him at half past eight,' he said. 'I'm afraid I can't stay more than fifteen minutes. I'd have rung you, only it seemed less rude to call round and make my apologies.'

Veronica put her head on one side and smiled sweetly. 'I thought you said you were going to stop seeing Charlie Evans?' she said.

'I'm sure I never said any such thing! It was you who said . . .'

'Don't raise your voice, dear. People will think we're quarrelling. And we're not, are we?'

'No, of course not.' As usual in argument with Veronica, Henry found himself entangled in irrelevancies. While he was disentangling himself, Veronica sailed serenely on.

'If you remember, I simply suggested that in the long run it's cruel to keep up these schoolboy friendships merely out of some mistaken idea of loyalty. And you agreed. You said yourself that it was becoming increasingly difficult to talk to him. I was only trying to save you from worse embarrassments in the future. Of course, it means nothing to me, but . . .'

Veronica shrugged, and Henry found his tongue. 'You don't seem to realise,' he said hotly, 'that Charlie and I are not just schoolboy friends, we went right through the army together, he's like a brother to me — closer than a brother — good heavens, I couldn't just *drop* him! Anyway,' Henry added, with daring defiance, 'he's still my only real friend in London.'

'That's not very kind, Henry.' Veronica looked down at her shoes, as if to hide the sudden glistening of tears. Henry started to bite the side of his thumb impatiently. 'You know perfectly well what I mean,' he said.

'I thought,' said Veronica in a low voice, still looking down unhappily, 'that we were all your friends here.'

Oh God, thought Henry, here we go. He would have liked to give a sharp answer to Veronica's plaint, but he did not dare. For all his hard-won independence from family, background, and the mad whims of employers, he was not yet far enough from being a raw, uneducated Welsh peasant (which was what he had felt himself to be when he first came to London) to escape a feeling that all these rich, powerful people could, if he offended them, throw him wantonly into gaol. His engagement to Veronica had given him a delicious sense of safety, but he knew now that this had been an illusion: they belonged, still, to different races. As he watched Veronica twisting her bony hands together, waiting for his apology, all his old feelings of exposure, danger, came flooding back.

'You know I didn't mean that,' he said awkwardly. 'I mean, he's my only friend outside your circle. I mean, well — I'm sorry.'

Veronica looked up, smiling brilliantly. 'That's all right, dear,' she said briskly, 'I knew you didn't mean it, you're such a tease. And I'm sure Charlie Evans will soon find someone else to drink with as soon as he realises you're not going to turn up. You take my advice and just stop seeing him, and I just *know* you'll realise how right I was after a little while . . .'

'Veronica!' exclaimed Henry. He was deeply shocked. For a moment he could not find words to express his sense of outrage. Veronica stared at him blankly.

'Well, what?'

'Veronica, you're not suggesting that I should just leave Charlie sitting there on his . . . sitting there, and — *and just not turn up?*'

'Well, why ever not? I suppose you're meeting him in that dreadful pub? From what I know of him I shouldn't think he'll break his heart. It's not as if you'd arranged to meet him in a shop doorway or something . . .'

'But, Veronica!'

'And what about me, anyway? You worry a lot about your drunken friends, but you don't seem to think I'm worth any consideration at all! You come here, smelling of beer . . .'

'Veronica!'

'. . . treating this house like a public convenience . . .'

'Veronica!'

It was one of the peculiarities of the Timberley world that they all seemed unable to avoid unfortunate conjunctions of words, so that Henry all too often found himself choking with silent laughter at wholly serious moments. So strongly did he feel now, however, about Veronica's suggestion that he should stand Charlie Evans up in her favour, that he scarcely noticed her newest phrase.

'. . . you haven't even asked me how I am or why I asked you here so specially tonight, no, you just want to go rushing back to your boozy pals . . .'

'Veronica!'

'Oh, do stop saying "Veronica!" like that, you'll drive me mad! Now for heaven's sake let's have no more of this nonsense, we're just wasting time. Mrs.

Ordovice has a Bible Class later this evening, she'll have to dash off soon and I *do* want her signature . . . Oh, I must go and get the letter, we'll do that first, you stay right here and don't move and I don't want to hear another word about your leaving!'

Veronica smiled indulgently on her last words, patted Henry's sleeve, and skipped away, leaving him rooted to the spot, not so much by obedience as by simple horror. There had been tiffs and disagreements in the past, of course. Sometimes Henry felt that Veronica's treatment of him was a little cavalier; even, perhaps, bossy; but being an unassuming young man with a modest view of his own rights, and possibly an inflated view of Veronica's intelligence and authority, he had found this only natural. But this evening, for some reason, everything was different. He was appalled at Veronica's attitude towards Charlie Evans; who was, Henry decided in a sudden flush of loyalty, the only real friend he had ever had. He looked again at his watch, more than ever determined now to leave at such a time that, had there really been an appointment with Charlie at 'The Onions', he would have been able to keep it punctually.

'Your dear girl has dashed away again I see,' said Captain Herbert, who had danced expertly around three walls of the room in order to arrive at this point at Henry's side. 'Such a busy little thing she is, always wearing herself out in some good cause. A real Christian, like all the Timberleys. My uncle, the Brigadier, always used to say of Sir Charles — Veronica's uncle, of course — that if he hadn't gone into politics he would have made a devoted missionary. I thought at one time I might have a vocation myself but I was persuaded otherwise. You know how it is . . .'

'As a matter of fact,' said Henry, 'I don't. I'm not a Christian myself.'

Captain Herbert chortled. 'Yes, yes, yes, you're quite right to rebuke me, my boy, one falls into spiritual pride so easily, one really ought not to boast of one's spiritual life. But do be careful, dear boy, who you say that sort of thing to. It's all right with me, of course, I can take a joke, but you know some people might take you seriously.'

Henry had always liked Captain Herbert. There was something appealing in the old pouf's gentle bewilder-ment in the face of his own failure to amount to any-thing in the world. Now he found himself looking at this grotesque little figure with different eyes: not with dislike, it was more positive than that: with unbelieving astonishment. How, he asked himself, had he come to be standing next to this insubstantial, irrelevant creature? What was Captain Herbert doing here? What were any of them doing here?

Henry looked briefly at each face in the room: Mrs. Timberley whispering urgently to Mrs. Ordovice, the plumes of whose hat (and why was she wearing a hat?) swept the air like scythes as she nodded her stern agreement; plump Philip, the publisher of chil-dren's books, cadaverous Mr. Winchester, the born orator, toothy Margaret Arcadia, writing a thesis, Aunt Bea standing like a golfer, thick legs apart, while she barked asthmatically at two bewildered-looking Indians who had suddenly appeared in the room, unannounced, apparently from between the window curtains; and poor Aunt Ada, staring into space with the glassy smile of the stone deaf from her wheel-chair near the door.

There was nothing specifically *wrong*, socially or politically, with the gathering, nothing one could put one's finger on and say, 'Here, *this* is the common denominator which makes all these people utterly strange and mad and intolerable.' And yet that is what Henry felt about them. It was true that he thought of himself as vaguely Left, and he knew that most of these people were vaguely Right; it was true that as the son of a Welsh market gardener who had read nothing but the Bible and *The Smallholder* throughout his life, Henry belonged to a different cultural and social level from everyone else present, including the Indians; but these distinctions might very often obtain in one of those public-house drinking groups in which Henry felt entirely at home. Henry knew, with one part of his mind, that these people were far more admirable than his pubby friends: they had social consciences; were diligent, responsible, and within their limits thoughtful; and yet there was something fundamentally wrong with them.

Henry felt himself to be not just a stranger, but a different type of living creature. He didn't know what these people were, what they meant or how he had come to be among them. He felt no animosity towards them. They inspired in him a consuming fear, and he felt that if he did not get out of this room as quickly as possible he would start screaming. Already, he noticed, he was beginning to tremble slightly. With an enormous effort he gained some small degree of control over himself, muttered an incoherent apology to Captain Herbert, and started edging around the room towards Mrs. Timberley.

At this moment Veronica appeared in the doorway, brandishing a sheet of paper. She stood there for a moment, looking around the room with a faint smile, as of some sensual anticipation; and then strode vigorously forward, calling for silence and attention, until she had reached the centre of the room; and there she took her stance, holding the piece of paper gaily above her head, while the murmurs died out around her and the loving smiles faded into proper gravity. Only poor Aunt Ada and the two Indians continued to smile. Henry suddenly realised with sickening apprehension that Veronica was about to make a speech. He looked at his watch. He would have to leave in eight minutes if he were not to keep Charlie Evans waiting.

'Friends!' said Veronica. 'You all know, I think, that this is not just a social gathering. Of course we are delighted to see any of you at any time, but tonight you have been asked here for a special purpose. You are all, every one of you, men and women of conscience. You know the difference between right and wrong. That is why we have asked you here. The ranks of your kind in the world today seem to be growing thin.'

At this point one of the Indians had a fit of coughing, and turned away to bury his face in a snowy handkerchief. The other said 'Hear, hear!' in an encouraging voice, and his smile broadened. Henry's heart warmed to him. Veronica smiled thinly in Henry's direction. She was standing between him and the door.

'I am sure,' Veronica went on, 'that you have all been as alarmed as I have at the course events have taken, during the past fortnight, in the Castillian Islands dispute. I think you will agree with me that our attitude towards these events need not be coloured by any political convictions we may hold. Many people are saying that what our Government has done is wrong because it is inexpedient, others that it is wrong for constitutional reasons, others that it is a transgression of international law. But while I respect the sincerity of these views, they seem to me to be, as usual, begging the question. I believe, and I think that most, if not all, of you agree with me, that the imposition of their wishes by one country or one person on another country or another person by the use of force is in all circumstances utterly unjustifiable.'

Veronica's voice, which had risen considerably in volume as she neared the end of her peroration, stopped dramatically; and after a moment's complete silence a soft wave of murmurs — whether of agreement or disagreement it was impossible to judge — lapped tentatively round the room.

'Excuse me, Miss Timberley,' said one of the Indians — the one who had had the coughing fit — in an apologetic tone — 'I don't wish to interrupt you, but I ask leave not to be considered in that conclusion.'

'Oh, you'll come round, you'll come round!' cried Veronica gaily, waving her sheet of paper at them in a comradely fashion. She then turned her back on them — and on Henry — so that she was facing poor Aunt Ada, and continued her speech.

'Of course, mine is the purely Christian position, as you all know — I don't see how any Christian can get round the fact that Christ endorsed God's Commandment against killing, Mark ten, nineteen — but of course there are other — many other — routes by which this little island of truth may be reached. My fiancé, for instance' — Veronica swivelled briefly on her heel, flung an arm at Henry, and at once turned her back on him again — 'my fiancé, who still has some verbal objection to calling himself a Christian, has served in the army, has killed men, and is now a pacifist. Our dear old friend Captain Herbert, a distinguished officer in two terrible wars, became a pacifist not primarily through his faith — though we all know him as a devout man — but through having seen, with his own eyes, how futile in the end is the use of force. I expect we all remember how Mr. Winchester nobly resigned from his post at the wartime Ministry of Information in protest . . .'

'Miss Timberley, oh, Miss Timberley,' cried one of the Indians, in some agitation, 'excuse me, I don't wish to be rude, but is it not that the Christian Church has no widely accepted doctrine on the issue of pacifism? I came not to send peace but a sword, Matthew ten, thirty-four. I am sorry, it is nothing. It is just that I am ignorant in this question.' The Indian smiled brilliantly, so that charming dimples appeared in his smooth, dark cheeks.

'Well . . .' said Veronica.

There occurred here a pause, an expectant silence in

which Veronica looked brightly and enquiringly towards Mrs. Ordovice, the acknowledged expert on such
questions, and Mrs. Ordovice frowned reprovingly
at the Indian. Henry, to his own surprise, suddenly
found himself speaking.

'You know, Veronica,' he said quietly, 'you mustn't
go on calling me a pacifist. I'm not one.'

'Oh, come, come!' said Captain Herbert jocularly.
Mrs. Timberley sighed loudly and laid a thin finger
against her cheek. Mrs. Ordovice sniffed, and the
Indians turned eagerly towards Henry, tense at the
delicious prospect of controversy.

'I beg your pardon?' said Veronica distantly.

'I said, I'm not a pacifist. You know that perfectly
well.'

'Oh, nonsense, Henry! You've always said you
were.'

'I never said I was.'

'You did. When we first met, and you'd just come
out of the army, you said you were never going to
fight again. And you've always agreed with me about
pacifism.'

'No, I haven't,' said Henry stubbornly. 'I've just
not disagreed, which isn't the same thing. I said I
didn't like killing people, that's all.'

'But that's exactly what pacifism's about!'

'No, it isn't.'

'Why isn't it?'

'I don't know. But it isn't.'

The Indian who had been ignorant about Christianity said 'Hear, hear!' in a low voice, but it was not
clear whom he was supporting. Veronica said 'Oh! ! !'

in exasperation; but then, with a visible effort, summoned to the lower part of her face a smile of almost overpowering sweetness, and turned to address the room at large. 'Dear Henry!' she said. 'Always such an old stickler for the precise form of words. Of course we all understand that one's deepest moral convictions are very personal things, and one does well to be chary of labels for them. I think in this case it is clear that Henry is frightened only of the *word*, not of the idea. Now we really must get on.'

'All the same, I'm not a pacifist,' muttered Henry; but only the nearer of the two Indians heard him.

'I have asked you all here tonight,' Veronica continued in ringing tones, 'to ask you for suggestions on what action we should take to make our views known to the Government and the public. This is an occasion we must seize with both hands, for many people will find themselves agreeing with us for reasons very different from our own, and this sympathy may lead them towards seeing the whole truth of our arguments. I have a few little ideas myself about how we can reach the public, but we must discuss those later. First of all, as a preliminary shot, as it were, across the Government's bows, I have drawn up a letter to *The Times* which I am now going to read to you. If you agree with the substance of it, I am then going to give each of you a copy of it and ask you to find signatories — not just anyone, but names that really *mean* something. I think that with Nigel Winchester, Philip Bosby, Lucy Ordovice, Margaret Arcadia, Henry Hywel Hughes, and, if I may say so without too much family pride, my mother, we have a nucleus of names which carry a certain weight. Captain Herbert, of course, is an enormous asset to us, having half a foot still, as it were, on the military side of the fence; and I may say that I have a half-promise — perhaps even a three-quarter promise' — Veronica gave a jolly, complicit smile to her mother, as if sharing some delightful secret — 'from Lord Tottenham, old Lord Mordrake's eldest son, to look in later this evening and see if he can help us!'

Mrs. Timberley beamed wanly through the white curtains of her hair, Aunt Bea blew her nose loudly into a khaki handkerchief of enormous size, and Mr. Winchester snapped his fingers and called sternly: 'The letter, the letter!'

Henry looked at his watch. He ought to be leaving, he was going to be late. His desire to leave was as strong as ever, but for the moment, apart from the physical and social difficulties involved in getting out of the room, he was prevented from doing so by a masochistic curiosity; a desire that the last vestige of his respect (if that's what it was) for Veronica should be finally and utterly swept away. That his relationship with her had this evening already reached its end he was already aware. He had publicly disagreed with her, and he knew that, even if he wanted it, he would not be forgiven. What he wanted now, now that the stucco had crumbled away from the fragile edifice, was to see the bricks falling, the foundations, in all their inadequacy, laid bare.

Veronica held her sheet of paper close to her eyes, as if she were shortsighted; and then held it out at arm's length, as if it were a proclamation written in two-inch black capitals. 'Well, friends,' she said, 'here it is. "Dear Sir . . ." '

'Miss Timberley, oh, Miss Timberley!' exclaimed the Indian who had quoted the Bible, 'if you are writing to *The Times* newspaper, you must just write "Sir", not "Dear Sir". It is a matter perhaps only of form, but if you wish your letter to be published I am sure you must not say "Dear Sir". I am sorry. It is nothing, of course, nothing at all.'

'You're thinking of the *Daily Telegraph*, old chap,' said Captain Herbert, smiling obsequiously. 'You can say what you like to *The Times*, you know.'

'Oh, now look here,' said Aunt Bea forcefully, 'the boy's quite right, you know, Captain. I read *The Times*, too, and I've always noticed most particularly that the letters all begin "To the Editor of *The Times*, Sir", and end up "Yours, etc.". I mean to say, if it's simply a matter of *fact* you can rely on me. I know I'm only a woman, but . . .'

'As a matter of fact,' said jolly Mr. Philip Bosby, speaking for the first time in, to Henry's astonishment, a broad Yorkshire accent, 'it dewsn't matter what you poot, they always alter it to suit their awn convention.'

'Thank you, Philip,' said Veronica, through her teeth. 'Shall I go on?'

'Yes, yes, yes, yes, yes!' said Mr. Winchester testily.

' "Dear Sir",' said Veronica firmly. ' "We, the undersigned, wish to protest most forcibly at the Government's actions in the Castillian Islands. As is no doubt immediately apparent, we are not all of one political persuasion, nor do we pretend to follow the arguments of those who object to the action on diplomatic grounds. No, what we are concerned about are the larger moral issues involved, issues which are, in the most literal sense, matters of life and death. The Castillian crisis is significant in a particular sense, in that no ideological confusions need enter into it. The matter is not one of ownership but of administration, and yet the British Government has seen fit to oppose the decisions of the legally elected leaders of these islands by a blatant show of force. At this moment, Sir, men, women and children are being killed in the Castillian Islands, wantonly deprived of this precious gift of life, mangled, maimed and bereaved, because our Government, still rooted in the nineteenth century, believes that bullets speak louder than words. We believe most profoundly that they do not. We believe that if mankind is to progress, both spiritually and materially, if indeed it is to survive at all, there must come a time when nations start refusing to win their arguments with this dreadful trump of death. Someone will have to give a lead. Someone will have to say: no, this has gone on too long, let us sit down together and talk. It is still not too late for the British Government to do that now. At the time of writing the situation is grave enough, but not yet irretrievable. By one single imaginative act on the part of our Government, it would be transformed overnight, and news of such action would ring round the world like a bell of hope. Are we never to hear that bell?" '

Veronica, flushed, uplifted, transformed by the power of her own words, dropped the paper to her side and let her eyes blaze round the room. There was a long silence, almost reverent in its intensity; and then the two Indians, as one man, suddenly cried out 'Bravo!' and started clapping, grinning and clapping, until everyone else in the room joined, a little diffidently, in the applause.

Henry found himself clapping too. He had been unexpectedly moved by Veronica's letter. Given that it was pompous, confused, a little beside the point, and composed in the sort of sonorous rhetorical periods that were anathema to him, it had yet moved him. He could not, as he had half hoped, despise her for it, nor doubt the warmth and sincerity of her feelings: which meant that, since he still felt the terror and revulsion which had overcome him just before the reading, there must be something basically wrong with himself. Why, oh why, was nothing ever *simple?* he mourned to himself. Now, more than ever, he wanted to get away and adjust himself to this new turmoil in his mind. He remembered Charlie Evans waiting for him in 'The Onions'. He was already late.

As after a fight, those who had stood back against the walls during Veronica's speech now pressed forwards to surround her. Mr. Winchester had taken the letter and was studying it with a frown, pulling irritably at the loose skin under his chin with the thumb and forefinger of his left hand. The Indians were talking excitedly to Mrs. Ordovice, and Margaret Arcadia was already in passionate argument with Aunt Bea on a point of order. Captain Herbert, apparently in tears, was the only person to observe Henry as he slipped out of the room.

In the hall Henry found Philip Bosby, who was

hunching himself awkwardly into a heavy coat with a fur collar. 'Oh, are you leaving too?' asked Henry unnecessarily.

'Yes, moost go, moost go, late already. What d'you think of it, eh? The letter?'

'It's obviously very sincere,' said Henry.

'Oh, it's that all right. Won't get pooblished though, not as it stands. Well, we'll thrash it out, eh? Thrash it out!'

Henry followed him back into the drawing-room and waited behind him as he made his apologies to Mrs. Timberley. When she saw Henry with his coat on, Mrs. Timberley drew herself up, as if to face an enemy.

'Henry! You're surely not leaving? Not *now*, just when Veronica needs you most?'

'I'm sorry, Mrs. Timberley, I'm afraid I must. I've already explained to Veronica, I had a previous appointment, it's absolutely . . .'

'I can't believe that Veronica knows about this, my dear, I'm sure she wouldn't let you go. *Veronica!* Veronica—— Oh, darling, come here, Veronica, surely Henry isn't leaving *now*?'

Mrs. Timberley contrived to inject into this last word not only extreme incredulity at Henry's lack of ordinary good manners, but also a sense of the moment's extraordinary significance, its unique promise; and a conviction that no-one, not even an uncouth Welsh peasant, could fail to honour the responsibilities that such a moment imposed.

Veronica made no effort to detain him. 'He can go if he wants to,' she said coldly. 'I can't stop him. If he thinks it's more important at a time like this to go and swill booze in some filthy pub than it is to help me here, it's probably better that he should go. Good night, Henry.'

Veronica left the room quickly, leaving Henry to twist his hat in his hands at Mrs. Timberley's side. He was aware that the room had fallen silent, that everyone, including the two Indians, was looking covertly at him, as if they knew all about him, could see plainly into the nastiest, most secret places of his soul. Already he could sense the pious sighs taking shape: Of course, he was never really *one of us*; Poor Veronica, she's done so much for him; It's probably all for the best, you can't make a silk purse out of a sow's ear . . .

'I must say, Henry,' said Mrs. Timberley faintly, after a long silence, 'I'm rather — *disappointed*.' She closed her eyes and turned wearily away. Henry, after a moment's hesitation, glanced once wildly round the room, and fled.

Chapter Four

WHEN Henry had denied to Veronica, and (which to her would be worse) in front of Veronica's friends, that he was a pacifist, he was aware that he was telling only an aspect of the truth. Yet it had to be said. Although he had never felt sufficiently confident of his own dialectical powers actually to challenge the pacifist arguments which Veronica had so often put forward, he had always avoided having to show a specific agreement with them. He knew that he was not a pacifist, in the sense that Veronica was one, because, faced with the basic arguments against pacifism, he could find nothing with which to counter them. Veronica could, and did. Perhaps it was necessary, he sometimes thought, to belong to a Great Power in order to believe in this absolute form of pacifism. But Henry was a Welshman, a member of a conquered, emotionally oppressed race. He knew in his bones that there were hundreds of millions of human beings in the world whose identities as members of this or that race were worth more to them than their lives; and to whom the thought of Veronica's pacifism would be one big belly-laugh. He did not think this — he knew it: in the same way that he knew that, ultimately, Veronica was right.

But for Henry abstract ideas had no existence. He

could not cope with theoretical ideals, only with practical ones, formed with the concrete images of his own experience.

When he had joined the army, Henry had not at all expected to be required to fight. Lance-Corporal Hughes and Corporal Evans had set off with their battalion for Cyprus in the same mood of hilarious schoolboy adventure with which they had approached the recruiting office; and there to his utter astonishment Henry had one day found himself, with the smells of cordite and orange blossom mingling in his nostrils, kneeling in the dust to fire at the running figure of a lean Cypriot youth some years younger than himself. It was a shot, as his sergeant had remarked kindly as they walked together towards the dying boy, which any experienced fighting man would have been proud to pull off.

Henry was not the material for martyrdom. Others, feeling as Henry felt, might have proclaimed publicly their renunciation of violence, might have seen fit to offer themselves, a mute symbol, to the awful vengeance of the British Army. Such behaviour would have been out-of-character in Henry. He could not believe that any gesture of his would stop people from killing each other, but he was perfectly determined, for his own peace of mind, to do no more killing. He realised that he ought to have known this from the start, for he had always shrunk from violence. It had been the rifle, which had enabled him to do violence at a distance, that had been the deceiver; just as, he now saw with terrifying clarity, the aeroplane had deceived many thousands of perfectly decent young men into murdering women and children whose existence they did not even have to imagine. There was some confusion in Henry's mind at this stage as to what other people ought or ought not to do in these matters, but it was quite clear that for himself one killing was more than enough to live with for the rest of his life. It was many months before he could close his eyes at night without seeing that lithe brown figure leaping away through the dusty vines, without feeling again that shock of incredulity as he leaned over the boy's twitching body and watched the meaningless film of death come up to cloud the puzzled brown eyes.

With his temperament, it was not difficult for Henry simply to avoid trouble, to shoot wide when shooting was in order, and to bear without resentment the gradual change from disappointment to scorn in his sergeant's manner. He lived out the last two months of his service in Cyprus in apprehension, but without any disastrous incident occurring, and returned to England, with only six more months to serve, determined never to fight again.

It was less easy to cope with Charlie Evans than it was to cope with the army, for Charlie asked questions. At this time they were still too close to each other, and to their shared boyhood, for either to have recognised that there was a fundamental difference between them: Charlie, despite his incomplete education, was an intellectual; Henry was not. Once he had divined Henry's state of mind, Charlie was determined not only to rationalise it, but to force Henry into accepting any number of distant implications, many of which were quite foreign to his nature. For the first time in their

friendship they came up hard against a complete road-
block in their communications. There was exasperation on both sides. Henry could not see why Charlie,
who was not himself inclined towards a pacifist
attitude, should want to make Henry adopt one;
Charlie could not see how Henry could renounce killing
without fitting the renunciation into a complete ethical
framework. It was a deadlock; and their continuing
comradeship was only made possible by a mutual and
unspoken decision to let the whole matter drop. This
was easier for Henry than for Charlie, who continued
to worry away at the subject long after Henry had
accepted as an ineradicable part of his character an
attitude which he could neither explain nor defend.

By the time he met Veronica Henry had learned to
keep his mouth shut when arguments for and against
pacifism were in the air. But it would have been impossible for him, in the face of Veronica's questioning,
not to admit that, for his part, killing was out. He
was able to avoid going further than that simply
because, like all her family, Veronica talked more than
she listened. He found himself able, at first, to go all
the way with her over the Bomb, the arguments for
unilateralism seeming, on the face of it, to be self-
evident. He marched with her to Aldermaston, ex-
periencing an exciting euphoria at finding himself for
the first time in his life a member of a large group who
all thought as he thought: there was a wonderful feeling
of security in being surrounded by strangers who
would all automatically accept him as one of themselves before he had even spoken a word. Henry,
limping proudly on to the field at Aldermaston, satis-

fyingly aware that he had composed two chapters of
the latest Peter Colchester adventure in his head
during the four-day march, felt strangely elated; at
peace with himself, and at one with his fellow men.

But on the second march, as to some tormented
nineteenth-century parson who had been secretly dip-
ping into Darwin, Doubt crept insidiously in. Not
doubt as to the sincerity of others — although the
behaviour of some gave ample reason to suspect it;
Henry's doubt was of a more serious kind than that.
He doubted if he were worthy.

Henry had somehow become separated from Veronica. One of the peculiarities of the March, for
Henry, was that, out of the ten or twenty thousand
individuals from every corner of the British Isles —
and from America, Japan, Turkey, Hungary — who
had come to join this march, Veronica should know
so many. It was as if she belonged to some vast secret
society, so secret that it had no name, so vast that it
could block the road from Chiswick to Kensington,
whose members, having nothing else in common, could
at one bugle blast be summoned together for a single
purpose. Veronica, tireless, exuberant, militantly un-
squashable, sped up and down the slowly moving
column, in and out of the banners, joining now this
group of Bradford trade unionists, now that chattering
party of Nottingham university students, finding everywhere a friend or acquaintance, introducing people,
making links in her endless semi-conspiratorial chain,
distributing leaflets, bullying for signatures, as at home
in this strange element as a lean brown trout should-
ering through the whirlpools of a mountain stream.

But Henry trudged on stolidly, usually alone. On the occasion of his initial Doubt a mousy middle-aged woman was limping along grimly beside him, bearing aloft a massive banner with the unexpected legend: 'Ban the Bomb WOKING LADIES SEWING BEE Ban the Bomb'. Henry could see no other ladies in the immediate vicinity who looked even remotely like Woking needlewomen, and wondered if the other members of the Sewing Bee would really approve of this public display of their name. But he was not tempted to ask her. Peter Colchester was in trouble with Krossov again in the malaria-ridden marshes (Henry hoped there were some) of Central Nigeria, and Henry hoped to have thought of a way out of his present predicament before the marchers stopped for lunch. But it was not to be.

Henry had grown used to the occasional catcalls and insults thrown at the marchers by spectators on the pavement; he was insulated against them by the solid mass of humanity in which he moved. Not so, apparently, the mousy sewing lady at his side. A group of handsome, well-groomed young thugs, leaning with obvious boredom against some churchyard railings, started shouting in well-rehearsed concert as Henry's section drew near: 'What about Hungary? What about Hungary? What about Hungary?' Despite the four or five pairs of healthy lungs behind this shout, it reached Henry only dimly, for a group ahead were chanting 'Ban the Bomb! Ban the Bomb! Ban the Bomb!' in a monotonous rhythm, and the Bradford trade unionists behind were giving their twentieth or thirtieth spirited rendering of 'On Ilkla Moor 'b'aht 'at'. But the little brown woman beside Henry was suddenly galvanised into an almost incoherent fury of riposte.

'Hungary? Hungary?' she shouted, pushing past Henry so as to have a clearer view of her opponents. 'Isn't it something like Hungary that's going to tip us over the brink into the — the — the nuclear holocaust, the end of the world? All you can do is stand there — stand there — you boys — you've no idea — you don't think—didn't I cry my heart out over Hungary too? Oh!'

She was crying now. The column had moved on, and the boys who had shouted lounged back against the railings, trying to laugh among themselves at having stirred up this passionate response. The column moved on, carrying this moment of embarrassment away from those who had caused it and would so soon forget it, but carrying Henry along beside it, unhappily aware of the tears that streamed down unchecked over the pouched unbeautiful cheeks of the sewing lady from Woking.

'Here, let me carry that for a bit,' said Henry, taking the incongruous banner from tired, willing fingers.

'I'm sorry, I'm so sorry,' she sniffed, fumbling for a handkerchief in the pocket of her grey pac-a-mac. 'I know I shouldn't take any notice, but — Hungary! I couldn't sleep, I could hardly listen to the News, it was such agony, and there was nothing we could do, nothing . . .'

She started crying again, remembering: something had touched her imagination as Henry's had once been touched by a dying boy in a Cypriot vineyard, she had died the deaths of the innocent in the streets of Budapest. Henry understood and was silent, forgiving her tears, although other people's grief is difficult to forgive. Trudging on now through the drizzling rain, with Henry carrying the banner of the Woking Ladies Sewing Bee, they were together as they had not been before. After a little while, when her tears had dried, his companion began without preliminaries to talk. She talked of her belief in the essential goodness of people, which only needed encouragement to reveal itself; of the imagined horrors of nuclear war, so ever-present in her mind that she could not look at her grandchildren, when they were asleep, without bursting into tears; of her fear of pride, which led men to commit extraordinary follies in the conviction that they were serving their gods; of her incomprehension of the utter indifference to impending doom which she saw on every side.

Henry, listening, was appalled. He had never felt nor thought like this. Looking at the faces around him, the beery trade unionists from Bradford, the serious students from Nottingham, the bearded guitarists from Soho, he began to suspect that beneath each jolly, confident or brash exterior was hidden some such imaginative, terrifying conception of what it was all about as was now being revealed by the dowdy little woman beside him. But he, Henry, had no such conception. He had hardly thought about the matter in such terms, having accepted more or less without question that any instrument capable of slaughtering the populations of whole cities at one blow ought, self-evidently, to be banned by everyone. But now, paradoxically, listening to all the political and military arguments for unilateralism, which he had heard before but not attended to, the practical counter-arguments of the multilateralists came flooding back to him, and he realised with a shock that was almost hysterical in its impact that he *did not know*. How could he, Henry Hywel Hughes, ex-corporal, writer of cheap thrillers, possibly reach any decision on such a complex question? The arguments on both sides seemed to him irrefutably sound. He was delighted that all these other people had thought it out carefully and decided that there was less chance of someone dropping a bomb if Britain hadn't got one than if she had. He was quite sure that their hearts were in the right place, their desires on the side of virtue, their actions admirable. But, since he couldn't possibly tell whether they were right or not, what was he doing marching beside them? He was an impostor, a fraud; he was unworthy.

Among Henry's few but cherished virtues he valued personal honesty most highly. Not wishing to be impolite, he carried the banner of the Woking Ladies Sewing Bee as far as Kensington Gardens, where the March rested for lunch; but then slipped unnoticed away, mingling with the crowds of sceptical, sympathetic and hostile spectators who had come to gape at a lot of people making fools of themselves in public. An obscure sense of fairness obliged him to walk painfully, by side roads, the rest of the way to Trafalgar Square. And there, standing on the rim of one of the fountains, he found Veronica, exultantly acclaiming the measured words of the famous people who had come to speak to the crowd from the plinth of Nelson's Column.

Henry said nothing about his Doubts to Veronica. It would have been a useless undertaking, for Veronica could not understand people who failed to make up their minds about perfectly clear-cut issues.

Chapter Five

Henry had been carried, on the Underground, as far as the Temple before he remembered that in fact he had no appointment with Charlie Evans in 'The Onions'.

He alighted from the train and stood wondering what to do with himself. He could, of course, telephone Charlie at the Boys' Club, but he was far from sure that he wanted to see his friend just now, with his mind in its present confused state. Then he remembered the thing that had been bothering him when he had been trying to work earlier in the day. Crossing to the other platform, he set off once more, fairly aimlessly, in the direction from which he had come.

Henry had only the haziest memory of his movements of the previous night, and none at all of the influences which had brought him, at closing time, to a bench under the trees on the Embankment, opposite Cheyne Walk. He cannot have been drinking in any of his usual pubs, for they were further north, in the sleazier reaches of the Fulham Road. The incident with the Irishman in Mooney's had been at the beginning of the evening, and was, as far as he could determine, causally unrelated to later events, whatever they had been. He remembered calling in at the Anglesey, and at Finch's; and, having found none of his friends in these pubs, moving moodily southwards towards the river. But why he had moved south, and at which pub he had ended up, escaped him entirely.

It was to the bench on the Embankment that Henry now made his way, vaguely hoping that some revealing association of ideas might take place. Emptying his mind, as he was sometimes able to do when the complexities of life became too much for him, he sat down on the edge of the bench and stared out sightlessly, past the bust of Ford Madox Brown, into the gathering river mists. He lit a cigarette, and hummed a little tune to himself, screwing up his eyes and smiling for no better reason than that he had succeeded in making his mind a blank. A loitering girl, seeing his smile, smiled back at him, because it is unusual and amusing to see a young man sitting alone on a bench smiling to himself; but Henry did not see her. After a while he leaned forwards, came slowly to his feet, and noted with distant approval that he was setting off towards the Albert Bridge. He still had no idea where he was going, but was now confident that inspiration would correctly guide him.

It seemed at first that he was wrong in this assumption. He passed the first two pubs with scarcely a glance, but, turning into the third without hesitation, was immediately convinced that he had never been in the place before. Many young men in narrow cavalry trousers, short black overcoats, and oddly curled little hats, stared coolly at him from their stances against the bar. A group of puffy-eyed blondes huddled together in a corner, sucking milky-green Pernod through lumps of sugar with the serious air of neophytes preparing themselves for the performance of some pagan rite. This was definitely not the sort of pub that Henry was used to. The bar was decorated with murals depicting tropical beaches on which lazed naked girls made proper by many wreaths of flowers; ferns in baskets hung from the ceiling, and three stunted palms, in pots, interlocked their fronds in such a way as to divide the room down its axis, parallel with the bar. On one side of the palms sat the blondes with their Pernod; on the other side stood the oddly dressed young men, with their beer. It seemed to Henry that some never-formulated law decreed that these positions were not interchangeable.

He moved uncertainly towards the bar, sure that he was in the wrong place but unable to leave without buying a drink. The bar-tender wore a white coat and a red and white spotted bow tie. He gazed over Henry's shoulder as he drew the beer, accepted payment without a word, and, returning with the change, continued to stare out blankly into the room as if the painted horizons on the walls were real. As Henry leaned there, sipping his rather tired glass of beer and trying to decide whether he could have been so drunk the previous night as to be oblivious to such odd surroundings as these, the barman, without altering the focus of his eyes, spoke.

'It's a bugger, isn't it?' he said.

Henry looked round, but there was no-one else the man could have been addressing.

'What is?' he asked.

'What is!' said the barman sarcastically, as if only a fool could have failed to divine his meaning. 'This here war our lot have gone and started.'

'War?' said Henry, blankly.

'War?' mimicked the barman. 'Yers, *war*. What else would you like to call it? People shooting at each other. That's war, isn't it? Bloody fools.'

'Not very clever,' agreed Henry vaguely.

'Not very clever!' The barman took his eyes off the horizon and transferred them, blazing, to Henry. He leaned forward across the bar, baring his teeth savagely. 'Criminal!' he hissed. 'That's what it is! Bloody criminal! What right do they think they've got, I'd like to know? It's always the bloody same. You know what I'd do, if I hadn't got a bloody family? Emigrate! And you know where I'd emigrate to? Eh? Russia! Yers.'

'Aha, I thought you'd say that!' said a fruity voice at Henry's elbow, triumphantly. Henry turned. A florid middle-aged gentleman with a neat moustache bristling under a pox-pitted nose was beaming warmly upon him. 'You heard what he said?' the man said happily. 'He'd like to go to Russia. Typical. Just what I was expecting. You hear one of these bods running down their own country, you can be pretty sure they'll turn out to be Commies.' He turned to the barman, who was once more scanning the painted tropic seas. 'I suppose you'd have liked us just to sit around on our fannies and watch those damned Castillians kick the old Union Jack into the sea, eh? Yes, I know your type, old chap, I know your type through and through. You're the sort that gave away India, and now you're busy trying to chuck over your responsibilities everywhere else. Well, I agree with you, old boy — Russia's the best place for traitors! Oh, I agree with you there!'

The man gave a great gust of laughter and nudged Henry with his elbow. Some beer spilled on to Henry's best suit. The barman, who appeared not to have been listening during the fruity man's speech, said very quietly and wearily: 'Piss off, will you? Just . . . piss off.'

The fruity man continued to laugh, as at some widely-shared joke. Without Henry's having noticed, a small crowd had now formed a semi-circle around himself and the barman's opponent, and within a few moments the dispute had become general. One of the narrow-trousered young men attempted to make a judicious public statement: 'I don't think one can quarrel with the *principle* of the action, but it does just seem that the *timing* was a little unfortunate. As I understand it, the Governor-General and the Prime Minister Designate . . .' He had no audience but was still trying to attract one when Henry, squirming his way backwards through the bickering crowd, had passed out of earshot towards the door.

He might as well go home, he thought, or at least move on to a pub where there would be someone he knew. Everyone seemed very excited about this new political thing, but Henry was not prepared to listen to any of them until he had read up the facts for himself, which he supposed he would now have to do. With the accumulation of new problems — Veronica, the Castillian business, uncomfortable thoughts of Charlie sparked off by that imaginary appointment — the irritating half-memory which had brought him to this unknown, unpleasant pub had dwindled into unimportance. It can't, Henry thought, have been much, or I'd have remembered more about it.

But as he drained his glass and turned to open the door a hand tugged at his sleeve, and an almost-familiar voice cried: 'Harry! My dear, it *is* you, isn't it? Yes, of course it is! Have you seen Bertie?'

Henry found that his arm was being hugged by a pale, fair creature of about half his size: a youth so small and tender that he might have been taken for a boy if it had not been for the elegance of his cigarette holder, the confident tilt of his well-groomed head. The name came at once: Vernon. A piece of luck.

'Hello, Vernon. No, I haven't seen him, I'm sorry.'

'Her, you mean,' said Vernon. He giggled. 'One does get so confused, 'specially with Derek and Albert and that lot calling *me* "she", the cheeky things. You feeling better tonight, dear?'

'Er — yes,' said Henry.

'You were a bit naughty last night, you know. All that hugging and kissing — no wonder Fred asked us to leave. Never mind. We all thought you were sweet, actually.'

For one awful moment Henry wondered if the hugging and kissing had been done with Vernon; but then there floated up, out of the mists of a drunken evening, the single dew-clear image of a young girl's face.

'Bertie?' he asked tentatively.

'Oh yes, well now, Bertie. She's in the Denmark. She said to tell you, if any of us saw you. That's what I stopped you for, actually, dear.' Vernon looked wistful, and glanced once towards the bar. 'Don't ask me to come, Harry. I'd love to, but I'm here with — someone.'

'What a pity,' said Henry, insincerely. 'I'm sorry, but — I've forgotten just how one gets to the Denmark from here.'

'You've what?' Vernon giggled again. 'My, you *were* far gone, dear. It's right here. Just opposite. *Much* nicer than this place. You off then? Give them my love. I'll join you later if — er — business allows.'

As Henry closed the door of the bar behind him, he saw Vernon move across towards the beer-pumps, where the fruity man who had quarrelled with the bar-tender was still leaning, deserted now by the disputing crowd which he had helped to form. As Vernon approached him the fruity man threw a fraternal arm across the youth's slender shoulders, and bent to whisper some jollity in his ear. The bar-tender stood as alone and aloof as when Henry had first entered, a Crusoe stranded among savages beyond hope of rescue. Henry shook his head at himself, wondering why he understood so little about the world.

The saloon bar of the Rose of Denmark had little to distinguish it from the bar Henry had just left. The murals were different — Palladian temples on pale grassy knolls — but there were the same baskets of ferns and, it seemed at first sight, the same young men leaning in supercilious poses against the bar. There was perhaps a shade more animation: a game of bar billiards was being played in grim silence at the far end of the long room, and at some tables to one side sat a group of scowling Chelsea artists, wearing, regardless of sex, wrinkled black jeans and voluminous woollen jumpers. Sprawled across their chairs and tables in attitudes of utter exhaustion, they were quarrelling quietly among themselves with the bitter vehemence of old enemies.

Henry ordered a Guinness, hitched his elbows over the edge of the bar, and scanned every face in the room with care. There was no-one here that he knew, he was quite certain of that. The women among the group of artists were of a type with which he was familiar, at a distance, in the Fulham Road pubs. One of them might stray, from time to time, into Henry's orbit; but would soon realise her mistake and drift away again. They were not for him. The other women in the bar were of a type common in Chelsea since it has become too expensive a district for real artists to live in: the clever girls who make a lot of money out of some activity peripheral to art, such as interior decorating, or the equally clever ones with artistic leanings who have managed to land well-salaried husbands, and who hope, each year with diminishing confidence, that something of the imagined Chelsea bloom will rub off on them if they live there long enough.

Not that Henry saw them thus. To him they were all just strangers, living in worlds he knew nothing about, as remote from his understanding of life as the Timberleys had at last turned out to be. Once such places as this had seemed to him romantic, full of promise, pulsating with the raw material of a full life. Now he saw them differently: not with understanding, simply with disenchantment.

Henry shuddered a little, working his teeth grittily together as he did when he was displeased with himself. He had been in London too long. The place was beginning to take on that nightmarish quality, in which every face looks maddeningly familiar, every sentence seems to have been said a dozen times before, every establishment to be a slavish echo of its fellows. This pub, now that he reviewed it dispassionately, was clearly no worse than any of his own locals, in which, because he had friends in them, he was always content to spend an evening. Nevertheless, it was ghastly. In it could be seen every possible manifestation of the Great Sin of London: waste: waste of time, waste of money, waste of effort, waste of imagination, waste of human ingenuity. Every bottle on the shelves was a symbol of the millions of pounds being spent monthly on the greatest waste of all, advertising. The horrible murals were a waste of talent, paint, and good wall-space, the customers were a waste of what must once have been good human material. Henry looked at his nearest neighbour, a paunchy but still handsome man in his early forties wearing a good grey flannel suit, a neat little paisley-pattern silk bow tie. He looked pleasant enough: probably a solicitor or doctor, he had just that touch of conscious distinction which marks off the professional from the business man. But looking into his face Henry could see that he was so bored he had almost ceased to exist: bored not only with the woman (probably his wife) he was talking to, but with everything he had done, thought, felt, eaten for years without number. Bored with work, bored with play, bored with beer.

If I don't get away from London soon, thought Henry, I shall become like that. It's time I had a holiday, did something different, met someone new;

I've started to forget that there *are* other worlds, outside London. But for one who lived on credit, with money already borrowed on a manuscript which dragged increasingly slowly towards its end, there was no possibility of sudden change. He was trapped.

With this thought, Henry drew himself upright, horrified at the very feel of the word in his mind. He had endured much, including hard work and hunger, to become self-dependent, free of interfering relations, free of employers, background, class, to be always ready, as he had once romantically put it to Charlie Evans, 'to move my camp at the first sign of plague'. Yet here he was — trapped!

Henry squared his shoulders, firmed his jaw. There was only one thing to be done when one was trapped: start gnawing fiercely at one's bonds. He was no stranger to hard work and economy; indeed, as he thought of the regime to which he must now submit himself, an element of pure joy once more re-entered his soul. He knew that he was lazy, amoral, and weak; but there was this lurking strength somewhere in his nature that would always save him — often at the last possible moment — from the downward drift that had caught and held the walking dead of Chelsea and Soho. The eye that five minutes ago had been surveying the world with such apathetic dislike now gleamed brightly and blindly, and a self-absorbed smile had settled upon his lips. Henry forgot his half-finished glass of Guinness, forgot once more, as he made with determined step for the door, his reason for having entered the pub in the first place.

The unseasonable sleet of early morning had been

an unlikely freak. Now the familiar warm drizzle of a London summer was falling silently from a solid sky. Henry stood clear of the pub doorway and lifted his face to the rain and the ribbon of cloud above. Among the coastal hills where Henry had been born one lived not under the sky but *in* it: a span of light from one horizon to the other that ruled one's life as effectively as the seasons rule the soil. A man standing in a field felt himself to be sticking up into the sky, might watch a cloud creep across the valley-head until it lapped his feet. Remembering this feeling, Henry knew that his good resolutions were more than a temporary reaction. Fifteen thousand words to go — say a week of black coffee and intense self-discipline. His agent would probably part with another £50, possibly more, as soon as the manuscript was delivered, and that would settle the rent and the grocer's bill. He could hitch-hike to Wales; Elwyn would give him a bed; they'd be taking the first load of hay about now; and then the shearing . . . If there was one thing Henry really detested it was farm work, but for the moment he had forgotten this; just as he had forgotten, as he strode off towards the King's Road, that, drunk or sober, our acts define us.

Chapter Six

ENRY was conscious, immediately he awoke the following morning, that something was wrong. At first it was impossible to place: a feeling of space, exposure, danger. He lay in bed with his eyes closed and one arm hanging over the side of the bed, fingers just brushing the floor. All at once the sense of strangeness resolved itself: his mosquito net was missing. He opened his eyes warily to confirm that this was so, and then closed them again hurriedly. Sunlight, he had seen, was streaming through his windows in an abandoned flood. As he huddled down into the bedclothes he was made physically aware of a further irregularity. He turned over with reluctance to examine the girl at his side.

Bertie was already awake. Her dark hair, clinging to the pillow like the tendrils of a cottage creeper, fanned out untidily around a face that seemed to have grown smaller and whiter during the night. She smiled when Henry turned to look at her, an almost frightened, almost apologetic smile, and tugged up the shoulder-straps of her crumpled petticoat in an automatically self-conscious gesture. Neither of them spoke.

Henry relaxed again, resisting thought. He lay with his head turned sideways, his face so close to the girl's that she was almost out of focus. For several minutes they examined each other minutely, with mutual gravity. Then Bertie pursed her lips into a soundless kiss. Henry smiled, and said: 'Thank you.' Then they returned to their grave study of each other's face.

As Henry's mind emerged reluctantly from the safe pastures of sleep, the impersonal enchantment of awaking with a girl beside him was qualified by apprehension. What complications now lay in store for him he had yet to discover, but as the events of the previous night fell one by one into place, he realised that whatever freedoms had been gained by letting Veronica out of his life had been more than balanced by letting Bertie in.

'Are you all right?' he asked, out of his thoughts.

'I'm fine,' said Bertie. She smiled in a small way, and added very quietly: 'I'm sorry I cried.'

'It was my fault. It never occurred to me——'

'Of course it didn't. It wasn't your fault at all. I was doing all the chasing, not you. And I knew I ought to tell you I was a virgin. I thought it might put you off, though. I only cried because it hurt. I didn't want to, I just couldn't help it. I'm glad now, though.'

'Are you really?'

'Yes.'

But a tear had formed at the corner of the dark eye nearest to Henry. He watched it swell and spill and trickle down her temple into the fine black hairs above her ear.

'You're crying now, though,' he accused.

'No, I'm not. I'm very happy.'

On the last word a smothered sob broke through.

Henry, his stomach hollowed by an emotion which might have been love, might have been sorrow or anger or selfish dismay, pulled Bertie's head against his chest and buried his own face in her hair. She shook gently for a little while in his arms, and then, calm again, pushed back to peer into his eyes once more.

'You're a kind man,' she said.

'No I'm not. I'm very selfish.'

'You're not. You're kind. You've got a kind face. I could see you had a kind face that first night, when Vernon picked you up. That's why I was chasing you.'

'But it was me that was chasing you, that night, before I got so drunk. You told me so yourself.'

Bertie shook her head in vehement denial. 'No, no,' she said, 'you've got it all wrong. It's true you asked me to go to bed with you. But you were already pretty tight then, and I'd already made it quite clear that I would, hadn't I?'

'I don't remember.'

'You were naughty, getting so drunk. Why did you get so drunk?'

'I don't know.'

But Henry did know, and quickly side-stepped the sudden chilling image of his ex-fiancée.

They lay in silence for a while, gently caressing each other's shoulders. Then Bertie said, mainly to herself: 'I'm a wicked, wicked girl.'

'Why?'

'I just am. You'll find out. I'd like to be good, but it's very difficult.'

'You mean, because of last night?'

'Oh, *no*,' cried Bertie passionately, sitting up and staring at Henry as if he had said something shocking. '*That* was good — or it would have been, if I hadn't cried. Most of it was super anyway . . . no, I mean *really* wicked. In my head. I *think* dreadful things.'

'Everyone does,' said Henry, speaking with the conviction of self-knowledge. 'It's the things you do that make you wicked or not.'

'You don't know,' said Bertie, her eyes wide and awed, 'you just don't know the sort of things I think. I *shock* myself, sometimes.'

'You mean, like wishing an aunt would die, so that you'd get some money?'

'That sort of thing. Only *much* worse.'

Henry looked at the ceiling and wondered indulgently what this innocent child could possibly class as 'wicked' — some sexual fantasy, probably, or a piece of common selfishness. He knew so little about her that such speculation died from lack of material: he could not visualise her life.

'Where do you live, Bertie?' he suddenly asked, out of these thoughts.

Bertie gulped, and said nothing. Henry, thinking that she hadn't heard his question, repeated it.

'That's just it,' said Bertie.

'Just what?'

'I mean, I know what you're going to think, and I've just thought it myself. That's why I said I was wicked.'

'Thought *what*, for crying out loud?' Henry, suddenly exasperated, turned again to stare at the girl, propping himself up on one elbow and frowning with deliberate, unnatural ferocity. Bertie shrank back into the pillows as if he might eat her alive. 'Well, you see,' she said in a hopeless voice, as if it explained everything, 'I don't live anywhere.'

'Eh?' said Henry.

Bertie repeated her words patiently, and continued to gaze at him with wide, expectant eyes.

Henry's mind ticked over slowly. When, at last, he had reached the right answer, he could find nothing to say. His brain teemed with questions, but they would all wait.

'There you are, you see,' said Bertie accurately, 'you're thinking that I only went to bed with you because I had nowhere else to go. Aren't you?'

'Yes. No. I don't know. Did you?'

It was Bertie's turn to stare at the ceiling. She seemed to be thinking carefully about the question. Finally she sighed, a long weary sigh. 'Oh, I don't know. I thought of it just now — I mean, I thought of *you* thinking it — so it must have been in my head somewhere. I know I wanted you from the moment I first saw you — you must believe that.'

'At least you're honest about it,' said Henry, unable to keep a chilly edge out of his voice. He had suddenly remembered all those good resolutions.

Bertie turned to him quickly, at once alert to his withdrawal. 'Oh, please don't be angry, *please* don't! I could have pretended, couldn't I? Only I don't want to pretend, with you. I could have said — oh, Camden Town, anywhere — and you needn't have known. I wouldn't stay, if you didn't want me to.

I'll go now, if you like. It's only that — I get so *suspicious* about myself, somehow. I can't remember actually thinking last night that I'd have to find somewhere to sleep, but it must have been in my mind somewhere, mustn't it, or I wouldn't have been able to think that you might think it, and so . . . Oh dear!' Bertie retreated into the pillow again, her head averted.

'Don't cry again, for God's sake!' said Henry roughly. He slid out of bed, wrapped the counterpane round his bony body, and padded across to the electric kettle. 'I'll make some coffee, then we can talk. I'm not angry. Did you hear? *I'm. Not. Angry!*'

He sounded angry, though, and looked angry. Bertie, trying to make herself so small that the bed would swallow her entirely, couldn't know that his fury was directed only against himself. Henry's original alarm at finding that he had a homeless waif on his hands had by now turned into self-disgust at what he considered to be a cheap reaction.

The familiar routine with the kettle, mugs and powdered coffee gave Henry time to sort himself out, and by the time he came back to the bed, carrying a pint of milk, some letters, and a copy of the *Daily Mirror*, he was smiling easily, and humming a jaunty little tune.

'Paper,' he said, throwing it and the letters on the bed. 'You can open the letters if you like. All bills, I expect. Do you eat breakfast? There's nothing here, I'm afraid, we'll have to go out. Coffee won't be a minute. Cigarette?'

Bertie's eyes followed Henry like a faithful gun-dog as he moved, chattering good-humouredly, about the little flat. She accepted a cigarette, and a light, without a word. Once, when Henry turned suddenly to look at her, he surprised her in the act of smiling secretly to herself. She caught his eye, and they smiled together, for different reasons. Henry suppressed an impulse to get back into bed. There was some talking and thinking to be done before either of them had any more fun.

He sat on the edge of the bed, waiting for the kettle to boil. Wrapped in the flowered cotton counterpane he looked — and was aware of looking — darkly romantic, in a Middle-Eastern way. For a moment he allowed himself to drift into a Peter Colchester mood: Bertie was Domenica, weak from malaria contracted in the swamps of the Congo (no — the Sudan? swamps? Upper Nile?) and somewhere in the vast deserts of silence outside their tent (mud hut? cave?) the drums of Krossov's savage supporters were throbbing their messages of hatred and destruction. What were his chances of getting this frail and fever-racked woman back to civilisation, with the river swollen to a flood by the ceaseless rains, and hostile tribesmen, whipped to an anti-imperial fury by Krossov and his agents, lurking behind every bush?

'What's this?' said Bertie. Plunging her arms beneath the pillows in an orgy of sensuous stretching, she had encountered Henry's potato-gun, and was now holding it up, the barrel pointing at Henry's chest.

'Don't point it at me,' said Henry quickly, still half submerged in his Colchester dream, 'it's loaded!' He took it from her, gently and carefully. 'It's a potato-gun,' he said. 'Watch.'

He aimed at the dartboard above the bed, and

squeezed the trigger. With a soft *plop!* a little cylinder of discoloured potato hit the board and bounced back onto the bed.

'Lovely!' said Bertie. She took the gun back, squinted along the barrel at Henry's chest, and said: 'Pow! Pow! Pow!'

'Put it back,' said Henry. 'You shouldn't point it at me. I know it's only a toy, but guns are dangerous, you mustn't get into bad habits.'

'I love you,' said Bertie, grinning. 'And the kettle's boiling.'

While Henry made coffee, Bertie dressed. Her clothes had been thrown, the night before, over the chair by Henry's desk; and as she pulled on her skirt and blouse she was examining with interest the typewriter, the ocarina, and the neat piles of manuscript.

'What's all this?' she asked. 'Are you writing something?'

'That's right.'

'What is it? Stories? Can I look?' Bertie peered over the bar of the typewriter and started to read aloud. ' "*Little bits of my body, he thought, scattered across half the world. Colchester pulled himself up sharply. He must be getting soft, allowing himself to think like that. He crawled out from under the mosquito net and padded on bare feet across to the table, intending to read through the report he had written for Brigadier McNeil. For a moment he stood staring at the bare table with blank incredulity. Then his knees weakened, just as if he had been sandbagged from behind. The report was no longer there.*" ' Bertie looked up, her eyes shining. 'Golly Moses!' she said. 'This is exciting! What's happened to the report, then?'

'Oh, Krossov's got it. He's the villain. But he hasn't had a chance to read it yet, and Colchester will get it back before he does. There'll be a bit of a scrap, I expect.'

Henry felt rather self-conscious, talking about his work like this. It had never happened before. Veronica had always dismissed his writing with humorous, slightly disapproving indulgence; his agent's and publisher's reactions were purely venal; and Henry had never met anyone who had actually read one of his books. His own pleasure in them, such as it was, he had by now come to think of as the pleasure derived from a solitary vice, for they were linked indissolubly with his mosquito-net fantasies. The sight and sound of Bertie reading something that he had written gave him, momentarily, the same sort of shock as he would have had if he had been caught masturbating. As soon as this passed, however, he became conscious of a new, never-before-experienced pleasure, and a sudden flush of interest in what he had been writing so laboriously during the past few weeks.

'Is it a book?' said Bertie.

'Yes. A book. Nearly finished, now.'

'Golly! You mean you've actually *finished* — or nearly finished — writing a whole book? Do you think it'll get published?'

'I don't see why not,' said Henry, trying not to grin. 'I didn't have any trouble with the other five.'

'The other *five*! You mean to say you've written five — almost six — books! And you never told me!'

'You never asked. It's just another way of earning a living, after all.' Henry carried two cups of steaming

coffee across to the desk and started to fiddle unnecessarily with the papers beside the typewriter, embarrassment and pleasure almost equally mixed in his
reaction to Bertie's wide-eyed admiration. 'Here.
Coffee. Sugar's here, if you want it.'

Bertie had by now discovered the book-case, and
the collected works of Henry Hywel Hughes. With
the Italian and Scandinavian editions, they made an
impressive row, even in Henry's eyes. Looking at
them now with, as it were, another mind — Bertie's —
he suddenly felt that he was the unwitting author of an
elaborate confidence trick. It didn't seem at all
credible that he should have produced such an *oeuvre*
in such a very short time.

'You look too young to have written all those,' said
Bertie, voicing his own thoughts. 'You must be
terribly rich?'

Henry laughed. 'That's all you know, my sweet,'
he said, finding himself, to his own alarm, adopting
an entirely alien *persona* (he had never called anyone
'my sweet' before). 'The truth is that if I can turn in
one of those every six months I can just about keep
body and soul together. Just now I'm way behind
schedule, and therefore stony broke. If I don't
finish this one within a week I shall be in the shit-
house.'

Bertie looked sideways at him, questioningly, and
Henry knew that she had detected the false notes that
he could hear himself. He smiled uneasily, patted her
shoulder as if to reassure her that all this was of no
importance, and moved back to the bed with his cup
of coffee.

'BRITAIN DEFIES U.N.' said the *Daily Mirror*. 'LUNACY IN HIGH PLACES.' Henry threw the paper aside, sipped his coffee, and opened one of his letters. It was from a schoolboy in South Queensferry who had detected fourteen factual mistakes, all concerned with air travel, in the most recent Peter Colchester book, *The Kara-Kum Experiment*. Henry replied to all such letters immediately and with great care, for he honoured his public; but this one would have to wait a little while. He was about to open another letter when, glancing up, he saw that Bertie was staring at him with astonished eyes. She had a copy of one of his books in her hands, and was handling it with the same reverent love as he had himself felt for his first novel.

'Golly Moses!' said Bertie. 'How wonderful it must be to be you!'

'Come here,' said Henry.

Bertie joined him on the bed, and for a few blissful minutes they abandoned themselves to kissing and cuddling. For the first time in his life Henry felt himself to be in control of a situation in a thoroughly adult way; and rejoiced in knowing that whatever name might be given to the emotion which Bertie aroused in him, it was at least, and at long last, a genuine and unique emotion. When at length he pushed Bertie away and sat back from her, holding her hands between his own, to begin his questioning, he felt calmly confident that, whatever her predicament, Henry Hywel Hughes was exactly the right person to deal with it.

The only surprising thing in Bertie's story was that

it was all so predictable. If it hadn't been for the obvious sincerity in her telling of it, and her clear conviction that nothing so dreadful or so silly had ever happened to a young girl before, Henry might have suspected her of having made it up out of a novelette-fed imagination. Her full name was Albertine Miller. 'A funny name, Albertine,' said Bertie. 'My Mum got it out of some book. She was always reading; we used to say she'd become a book one day, the way she went on . . .' The mother was a widow, bringing up five children on the income from a tiny sweet-and-tobacco shop in deepest Somerset. Bertie, showing some talent for drawing and a conspicuous sense of colour, was sent, at fifteen, to a school of arts and crafts in Bath, where she learned some commercial art techniques and specialised in interior decoration. After two years of training she came to London to earn her fortune.

At first everything went swimmingly for her, success seemed assured. An introduction from one of her teachers to a fashionable decorator called Cecil Coburg secured her a job at what she considered to be a fabulous salary. Although she was given very little responsibility she enjoyed the work, and was always meeting (she said) 'terrifically interesting people'. But Coburg, who for professional reasons had sedulously cultivated a reputation for being homosexual, had in fact a different perversion: one involving immature girls, of whom Bertie was only the most recent in a very, very long list. Her rejection of his proposals was followed, almost immediately, by the sack; the 'terrifically interesting people' suddenly became inaccessible; other interior decorators, including those who, when she was in favour with Coburg, had attempted to lure her away, mysteriously found themselves over-staffed; Bertie's bed-sitting-room, which had seemed inexpensive while she had a salary, quickly gobbled up her tiny savings; and within a fortnight of her dismissal she found herself not only penniless, but roofless, friendless, and on the very brink (she said) of prostitution.

From this too conventional ending she was saved by Vernon, who, to Henry's astonishment (he seemed so ethereal a creature), turned out to be a specialist in fancy wrought-iron work, and was sometimes employed on a free-lance basis by Cecil Coburg. Vernon, himself a queer of the gentle, down-trodden type, had every reason to sympathise with Bertie, for he had once taken Coburg at his face value and had suffered one of those ego-shattering humiliations to which his type are so prone. He had not, according to Bertie, hesitated about offering to put her up in his own chi-chi little flat, had insisted on vacating his bed in her favour, and had been supporting her for the past fortnight while she searched, unsuccessfully, for a job.

'Queers are nice,' said Bertie. 'You know where you are with them.'

Unhappily for Bertie (and, in her opinion, for Vernon too) Vernon's lover had then returned from a business trip abroad, and had been understandably annoyed at finding Bertie in residence in Vernon's flat. It was at this point in Bertie's recital that Henry began to fit together pieces of the jigsaw which he had not previously grasped. He understood now why Vernon had picked him up on that first unfortunate night; and whence had come that obscure feeling of guilt the next morning. Drunk as he was, he must have apprehended that something more than casual friendship was being mutely asked of him; that in some indistinct way he had, by getting drunk, failed his new acquaintances. He must have been a sore disappointment to Vernon, he reflected; and turned once more to examining Bertie's innocent, eager face. He was pleased to detect in himself no trace of anger at her patently disingenuous confession of 'wickedness'.

'And so you see,' said Bertie, 'when you didn't turn up the next night at the Denmark, I went across the road to tell Vernon that I'd found a job, and a room, and that I wouldn't be sleeping at his flat that night. It wasn't true, but I couldn't go on spoiling their fun like that, and I thought it wouldn't hurt me to go and sleep on the Embankment — lots of other people do, you know. So then Vernon told me he'd just seen you and sent you to the Denmark — we must have passed in the street — and that's how I came to meet you just as you were leaving. And when I *did* see you — I nearly turned round and ran!'

'Why?' asked Henry, genuinely puzzled.

'You looked so fierce. And — and *untouchable*! Of course, I didn't know you were an artist then.'

'I'm not,' said Henry firmly. 'I'm just a writer of adventure stories. As a matter of fact, when I met you I was thinking about money, I expect that's why I looked so grim.'

Henry tried to reconstruct, as a matter of interest, the mental state he had been in the night before, immediately prior to meeting Bertie. But it all seemed a long time ago, life had changed since then. He no longer had the slightest desire to go to Wales.

'Are you angry with me?' Bertie asked. 'I wouldn't blame you a bit, if you were angry. It all sounds so terribly cold-blooded, but it wasn't really like that, you know. I honestly fell for you the moment I saw you. You can ask Vernon, if you like. He had to put up with me blubbing all night, because I thought I'd never see you again.'

'It doesn't really matter now, does it?' said Henry. 'You're here, that's the main thing, never mind what went on before you got here. I think we'd better start thinking about food.'

Henry stood up, threw off the flowered counterpane, and started dressing. Bertie continued to sit on the bed, gazing at him with adoration. 'The thing about you,' she said at last, 'is, you're not proud. It does save so much trouble.'

Henry was in the bathroom, shaving, when the telephone rang, so Bertie answered it.

'Hello,' said a man's voice. 'Who's that?'

'This is Bertie Miller,' said Bertie. 'Who's that?'

'This is Charlie Evans,' said Charlie. 'Is Harry there?'

'Harry? No—— Oh, sorry, you mean Henry. Yes, hold on, I'll get him.'

'Wait a sec,' said Charlie. 'Listen, has Harry opened his mail yet?'

'I don't think so. Why?'

'Is he in the room?'

'No, he's shaving. Hadn't I better get him?'

'Can you tell me if there's a long buff envelope from the War Office among his letters?'

'I don't know, I'm sure,' said Bertie, getting flustered. 'I really think you'd better talk to Henry — Harry.' But as she was sitting on the bed, with the envelopes scattered across the blankets beside her, she nevertheless rummaged among them until she found one that tallied with Charlie's description. 'Well, as a matter of fact there is, I've just found it now. But what is all this, anyway? I suppose you'll ask me to open it next? And I don't even know who you are!'

Bertie heard a snort of laughter, and was about to say something rude when Henry's face, half of it lathered and the other half streaming with blood from a multitude of tiny cuts, peered apprehensively round the bathroom door.

'Henry's here now,' said Bertie into the telephone, 'you'd better talk to him.' She held the instrument out towards Henry, and they both heard Charlie's voice saying: 'Tell him to read that letter, that's all. I'm coming round. Twenty minutes. Tell him to read the letter.' Click.

'Charlie!' said Henry.

'That's right.'

'What's this about a letter?'

Bertie held up the envelope, saying nothing. She had already noticed that it was addressed to '2357490 Cpl. Hughes H. H.'

Henry emerged from the bathroom slowly, dabbing at his face with a blood-stained flannel. He opened the envelope and read its contents in silence, then handed the papers to Bertie without a word. Under the Emergency Regulations such-and-such dated such-and-such, Bertie read, and in view of the present Emergency arising out of the disturbances in the Castillian Islands, Reservists who still had three months or more to serve on the Reserve were being recalled to the Colours, and 2357490 Cpl. Hughes H. H. was therefore required to report for duty . . . there was a lot more about next-of-kin, pay, compensation and travelling expenses which Bertie did not bother to read. She looked at Henry blankly, and Henry looked blankly back at her.

'And where the bloody hell,' said Bertie, 'are the bloody Castillian Islands?' Then she collapsed, weeping, across the bed.

Chapter Seven

Henry was lying on the bed, still only half-dressed, when Charlie arrived. He had been playing darts against himself in order to avoid having to think, but it had proved a useless ruse. His opponent (Colchester, who was usually allowed to win) hadn't even been able to get a double to start; the game lacked interest, and Henry's eyes had strayed again and again to the newspaper on the bed. 'LUNACY IN HIGH PLACES' — the enormous black letters covered half the front page. After ten minutes, with Colchester still unable to start scoring, Henry settled down on the bed to see what he could discover about this particular new lunacy.

He didn't discover very much. The front page told him that whatever Great Britain had done in the Castillian Islands had incurred the odium of the rest of the world, including the *Daily Mirror*. A resolution in the Security Council of the United Nations, calling upon Britain to stop whatever it was doing, had been vetoed by the British delegate, an act which the newspaper described as a 'cold-blooded slap in the face' for the friendly nations who were attempting to avoid an open breach in the Western alliance. Those of the inside pages which mentioned the affair concentrated almost entirely on Britain's historical and constitu-

tional position in the islands. None of this made much
sense to Henry. On one page there was a large photo-
graph of some barbed wire across a narrow street.
There were some bundles of old clothes lying around
untidily behind the wire. The caption said: 'AFTER
THE CARNAGE — the scene in Washington Street
at noon on Bloody Sunday.' When Henry realised
that the bundles were in fact corpses he looked away
quickly, as if caught in the act of watching a woman
adjust her stockings. He could find no mention of
Washington Street, or 'Bloody Sunday', elsewhere in
the paper.

If Charlie had asked him what he was doing, Henry
would have said: 'Thinking.' In a sense this would be
true; but Charlie, interpreting the word according to
his own use of it, would have had a very inaccurate
picture of what was actually happening in Henry's
brain: the succession of involuntary images pushing
against each other like lantern slides, producing new
images, sometimes blending into each other, sometimes
pushing each other apart, making patterns, dissolving,
re-forming in different patterns, always moving, circ-
ling, like a dog on a cushion, unable to settle to
rest.

A youth running, and then lying suddenly, inexplicably still: 'Oh, bloody good shooting, Taffy!'

A Regular Army sergeant, his forearm covered by
a score of tiny, tattooed skulls, each representing a
death: 'my life's work', he called it, grinning.

A mousy woman from Woking, crying uncontrol-
lably as she remembered the last days of October 1956:
'There was nothing we could do, nothing.'

Veronica, paradoxically ennobled by her own passionate conviction: 'Our Government believes that bullets speak louder than words.'

Emrys Pugh, Garth Foel, wiping the blood from his nose with the back of his hand after a fight, unwilling to get to his feet in case he should be knocked down again: 'It was supposed to be a *joke*, Hughes, honest to God it was only a *joke*!'

The English commercial traveller who took Betty Williams's cherry in the sheep pen on Ynys-fach when she was drunk on cider and fast driving: 'Be your age, old man. She was screaming for it.'

The quiet, leathery old man in Famagusta who would not be paid for the wine they had 'requisitioned': 'I don't take British money.'

Helena Soumopolosis, on the beach near Cape Greco, after making love: 'There are only three races — men, women, and children.'

Helena surveying the bomb-damage on the terrace of her parents' home: 'It was meant for me, of course.'

Elwyn's father looking down on the smooth green island of fields in its surrounding sea of snarling brown bracken: 'It's taken a thousand years to carve this farm out of the hills, Harry bach.'

Toni Zammitt, with a letter in his hands and a funny half-smile on his face: 'I must go back to Malta. It is necessary to kill my wife.'

'You got him, Hughes, you got him! Oh, bloody good shooting, Taffy!'

'. . . a better target for a kiss.'

The door was unlatched, and Charlie let himself in, grinning hugely as soon as he saw Henry. 'Tired, are

you, mochyn-bach?' he said solicitously. 'Must've
been working too hard. You want to take it easy.'
He looked all round the room ostentatiously, and
whispered hoarsely: 'Are we alone?'

'She's gone out to buy some breakfast,' said Henry.
He was trying hard not to grin, but couldn't stop himself. The mere sight of Charlie had always been
enough to make him squirm with pleasure; at this
moment he would have liked to have hugged him out
of sheer gratitude to him for existing at all. Charlie
was a small, solid, ugly man, the deep creases of his
face seeming to have been squeezed permanently into
place by some exterior force, as if he had just been
born. When he grinned, his eyes disappeared entirely.
His ears were of a peculiar size and thickness, and
stuck out from his head in that irrelevant fashion one
associated with bad sculpture; they could move inde-
pendently, both involuntarily and at will. In youth
he had been overconscious of his physical defects, and
had tended to exaggerate them deliberately as a form
of insurance against insult; later, finding that people —
including women — were attracted to him despite his
looks, he stopped worrying; but the habit of exaggera-
tion remained. Henry suspected that he half-deliber-
ately chose clothes that fitted badly and soon looked
old; just as, now, he probably relished the fact that the
beer bottles in his jacket pockets made unsightly
bulges, and strained the buttons of his coat almost to
breaking point.

'Didn't know you were married, old fruit,' said
Charlie, throwing the bottles on the bed and his coat
across a chair. 'Who was best man? Captain Herbert?'

Charlie knew enough about the Timberley set-up for this remark to eliminate the need for explanations.

'Shut up,' said Henry. 'Sit down. Let me look at you. You're getting old. Drinking too much?'

'Get stuffed.'

'You can come to my wedding, if you like. It's tomorrow.'

'Oh? When was this decided?'

'Ten seconds ago.'

'I'll come,' Charlie promised, 'but not tomorrow. Have to postpone it. We're off to Bont Newydd tomorrow, you and I.'

'How so?'

'Sheep shearing. Shortage of labour. Your country needs you.'

'You're telling me it does!' said Henry, remembering why Charlie was visiting him. 'I suppose you've had one of these things too?'

Charlie grinned, but said nothing. He left the bed to search for cups for the beer, and when he came back he was no longer grinning. Henry watched him expectantly as he poured the beer down the sides of the cups, frowning intently over the task.

'Good health to all Welshmen,' he said in Welsh, raising his cup.

Henry gave the ritual reply: 'The Devil's arsehole to all Englishmen.'

'And up it,' said Charlie, grinning again, 'they can stuff their putrid little war.'

'You mean you're not going?'

'Are you?'

'Well—— I hadn't really thought about it. I only opened the letter half an hour ago.'

'You must have seen it coming. It was announced days ago.'

'I don't read the papers, you know that, Charlie.'

'You crease me,' said Charlie. 'You really do. You lay me up. You're the most ignorant and lazy bastard I've ever met. If I hadn't known your Da I'd suspect you of having English blood. Jesus 'n Mary, here we are in the middle of . . . '

'Ah, wrap up!' exclaimed Henry. 'Look at you, blaspheming all over the place, and you a Minister's boy. Just give me the story, nice and simple, we'll have the pi-jaw for pudding.'

So Charlie told him the story. In his words, it didn't sound very unusual: just another of the mad, bad things that people were inexplicably doing to each other all over the world. But to Charlie, the details were all of vital importance: the constitutional manœuvrings, the votes and counter-votes, the resolutions and declarations, the discreet military moves, the timing and cause of the first shots, all added up, for him, to a pattern of immense and controversial significance. 'Show me a man who thinks what we've done is right,' said Charlie fiercely, 'and I'll show you a gun-boat Tory. This has separated the sheep from the goats, all right. Either you're on the side of humanity, or you're on the side of your own interests, first, last, and all the time. You can't have it both ways. What's sauce for the goose . . . Holy Christ! We spend years trying to build up an image of ourselves as a people with firm ethical standards, giving it

high and strong and pious to anyone else who mis-
behaves, and then as soon as there's a real twitch at
our own tail we start behaving like wild animals!
It's tragic, Harry, really tragic!'

Henry could see that, to Charlie, this was literally
true. He had had a hope, and it had been destroyed;
he had had a tentative pride, and it had been taken
from him; he had imagined an evolving pattern for the
future which could never now be completed. Every
word that he spoke quivered with outrage.

But Henry, never having entertained hope for the
world, pride for his country, or a vision of the future,
was unable to do more than sympathise. At one point
he even attempted to argue with Charlie's basic
precepts:

'But, look here, Charlie, are you sure you know all
the *facts* about this business? I mean, surely the
Government is more likely to know what it's doing
than you are? After all, there must be all sorts of inside information that never gets into the newspapers —
you only see the top of the iceberg. Isn't it possible
that the whole thing might look a bit different to you
if you could see it all?'

Charlie sucked at his pipe and squinted sideways
at Henry as if he had done something unpleasantly
out-of-character. 'A good question, Corp'l Hughes,'
he drawled. 'Also, if I may make so bold, a bloody
stupid good question. When Father Smith comes
reeling home from the pub, in a bad temper because he
lost a side-bet on a darts game, and has a quarrel with
Mother Smith, who's also in a bad temper because she
can't make the housekeeping money stretch far enough

to buy the kids some new shoes, and they have a quarrel, and Dad fells Mum to the floor with his big coal-heaving fist — do you think the neighbours, or the kids for that matter, ask themselves who was in the right and who was in the wrong? Do they hell! They say: "That Smith's a bloody bully, he ought to be locked up." And they're damned right, too!'

Charlie's eyes, wide open now, blazed with conviction. Henry, whatever he privately thought, didn't question his precepts again.

'The fact is, old fruit,' said Charlie, more gently, 'that in this case there aren't any parts of the iceberg you can't see. It's all been made hideously plain and public. There was a moment when our Government faced a perfectly simple choice which everyone understood. The issues were all perfectly clear. They had to decide whether to use force, or whether to appeal to the U.N.; whether to act according to our principles, or whether to betray them. It's as simple as that. I know that nothing I can do is going to make the slightest difference to anyone, but I'll not have any part in it, and that's that.'

They drank their beer in silence for a few minutes. Charlie was in no hurry now. He had said what he had to say, and had no need to elaborate it. For him, as for the Government, the choice was clear.

'You mean,' said Henry slowly, assimilating the idea, 'you're not going to report to Catterick at all?'

'You've got it, son.'

'That makes you a deserter?'

'That's right.'

'Won't they catch you?'

'They might, if I stayed down in Rotherhithe. But I don't see why they should come looking for me at Ty Coch.'

Ty Coch, the mountain farm which their schoolfriend Elwyn managed now that his father was immobilised by arthritis, was fifteen miles away from Blaengwyrionedd, where they had all been at school. Charlie's father, once the Minister at Sion Chapel, had retired to mid-Wales. There was nothing to connect him with Ty Coch.

Henry's parents were both dead. There was nothing to connect him with anywhere in the world.

'I'd better come too,' said Henry.

'Da iawn, cydymaith! I thought you would, once you knew all the facts . . .'

'It isn't,' interrupted Henry, 'anything to do with the facts. I dare say you're right, from your point of view, but none of that means much to me. You know why I can't report to Catterick, don't you?'

Charlie grinned. 'You're a stubborn old bastard, aren't you?' he said. 'All right, have it your way. I thought you'd grown out of all that, but as long as it means you'll come with me I'm not going to argue. So. Bont Newydd, tomorrow. Ten-ten from Paddington. Right? Can you cover your tracks?'

Henry's head began to spin: bills; milk; bread; rent; accommodation address for agent; money.

'I shall need some money,' he said.

'How much?'

'Twenty pounds would settle my bills and pay a month's rent in advance. I've got this room unfurnished, and it's cheap. I don't want to let it go.'

'Don't be daft, man! You can't keep it, you'll be traced.'

'I know that. I'll give up the lease, but Bertie can take it over. I shall still have to pay the rent, though.'

'I'd forgotten Bertie Miller.'

'I hadn't.'

Charlie opened more beer, and for a few more minutes they discussed the various complications of the move. Since neither of them could predict how long the emergency might last, nor knew what efforts might be made to find them, it was difficult to plan with confidence. Finally it was agreed that Charlie would lend Henry fifty pounds, so that he could settle his bills and give Bertie enough for rent and subsistence. Bertie would be given a fictitious forwarding address in Spain, which she could give to any suspicious-looking enquirers, but would in fact forward his letters to Ty Coch. There seemed no way of arranging things so that Bertie need not know the Welsh address.

'If it looks like being a long business,' said Henry, 'I shall have to send for her to join me in Wales. Then we shall have to think again.'

'You're really serious, aren't you? How long have you known this girl, Harry?'

Henry waved his hand vaguely. 'Oh, ages. I've only just come to my senses about her, that's all. This move's going to be a bit of a shock to her, I'm afraid.'

Henry had no sense of lying when he said this; he already thought of Bertie as his wife, and as someone whom he had known for years.

'So poor old Veronica got the push?'

'Oh, I broke with her ages ago. Ah, here's Bertie now.'

But it wasn't Bertie who opened the door, it was Veronica. Bertie, looking bewildered and a little frightened, came close behind her, loaded with parcels of food.

Veronica came to a halt just inside the door, barely leaving room for Bertie to squeeze past, drop her parcels on the bed, and quickly efface herself in the furthest corner of the room. Charlie rose, with a polite greeting for both of them. Bertie gave him a nervous grin, but Veronica did no more than nod in his direction, if that. She had screwed herself up to speak to Henry, and was not going to be deflected by social considerations. When she first came to rest inside the room she had stood with legs planted firmly apart, arms akimbo, like a truculent fish-wife; but, clearly feeling that this was too dramatic a pose to be kept up, she experimented for a moment or two with arms and legs and ended with a compromise: arms folded and feet together. It was not, Henry noted with compassion, a very successful combination.

'Henry!' she said.

Henry looked, and felt, both guilty and incredulous: surely she wasn't going to start a scene in front of the others? One of the attractions of going to Wales was the thought that he could write *FINIS* across the bottom of their relationship without actually having to go through a full-scale emotional show-down.

'Henry,' said Veronica again in her high voice. 'Have you been recalled to the army?'

'Yes, I have, as a matter of fact,' said Henry, trying to keep his voice easy and genial. 'So has Charlie.'

'I see. I take it you're not going?'

Henry glanced at Bertie: her wide eyes, glued to Veronica's face, registered something that might have been astonishment, might have been pure hatred. There was a little silence; and then Charlie gave a snort of incredulous laughter and said: 'Of course we're going. We're under orders to go.'

Veronica ignored him. 'Can't you speak for yourself, Henry?'

Henry, just in time, had seen the point of Charlie's move. 'Charlie answered you,' he said. 'We have to report to Catterick tomorrow. We're going together.'

'And what,' demanded Veronica through her teeth, 'about your pacifist convictions?'

'I've always told you I wasn't a pacifist. It was you who called me one, not me. I simply told you I couldn't kill anyone, but that needn't stop me from going in the army. It's quite easy to avoid shooting people.'

'That isn't what you've said before.'

'It's what I'm saying now.'

'You're a coward, Henry.'

'Oh no, he's not!' said Bertie suddenly, much too loudly. Everyone turned to stare at her. She coloured up, dipped her head once in automatic shyness, and then squared to the attack. 'How dare you just walk in here like that and accuse Henry of being a coward! How can he be a *coward*, anyway, if he's joining the army again? He might be a coward if he wouldn't,

if he was one of these whatjemecallits, conchies. But
he isn't, and he's been called up, and he's going.
What's cowardly about that, I'd like to know?'

Veronica looked at her with the interest one extends
to a new variety of beetle. Charlie was grinning, nod-
ding his encouragement to Bertie, only just able to
keep himself from laughing aloud. Henry, not at all
amused, tried to pretend that he wasn't there; or that
he could take only the most academic interest in the
discussion, which really couldn't have anything to do
with himself.

'I don't know who you are, young woman,' said
Veronica carefully, 'nor what you're doing here, but
you clearly have no idea what we're talking about so I
advise you not to interfere in matters you don't
understand.'

'Oh, now, look here . . . !' said Henry weakly.

'And I don't know who you are, old girl,' blazed
Bertie, 'or what the hell right you've got to come
busting in here, but I do know you're the damned
rudest person I've met in ten years! And I do *so*
know what I'm talking about! You can't go calling
my man a coward and get away with it, not while
I'm around you can't!'

'Oh, well said, Bertie!' cried Charlie, applauding.
Henry, quite unnerved, steeled himself for explanations,
apologies, recriminations. Various tentative phrases
hovered on his tongue, but he was not quick enough
to bring them forth.

Veronica, maddeningly but predictably, met this
outburst quite perfectly: *if only*, Henry mourned to
himself, *she would behave abominably, it would all be so*

much easier. 'I'm so sorry,' she said, in polite, if distant, tones, 'I didn't realise he was "your man". As he hadn't informed me otherwise, I was still thinking of him as my fiancé. Obviously I was wrong, but that's really nothing to do with the discussion. *Your man,* as you call him, is in fact a pacifist, and it's his duty to his conscience, and to everything he believes, to resist this call-up, even if it means going to gaol. The easy thing for him to do is simply to do as he's told, join the army, and keep carefully in the background if there's any fighting going on. That's the easy, *cowardly* thing to do. The difficult, brave thing to do would be to state publicly that he won't have anything to do with this stupid war, or any other war, and accept the consequences. But it seems he hasn't the guts to do that.'

Bertie, biting her lower lip hard because she was on the verge of tears, was unable to reply: and Henry was so stupefied at the nastiness of his own character that he could think of nothing to say at all. Only Charlie remained buoyant.

'That's all very well, Veronica,' he said cheerfully. 'If Harry was really a pacifist, you'd have put the situation in a nutshell. But he isn't. You've just heard him say he isn't, and I've heard him say so more times than I can count. We all know that you are, and I'm sure we respect your views even if we don't agree with them. You'd be quite justified in trying to convince him, as I'm sure you have in the past; but if you can't, then surely he must act according to his own conscience, not according to yours?'

Veronica, who had listened to this unnaturally long

speech with bowed head, now raised her eyes and addressed Henry as if Charlie had not spoken.

'I don't know, Henry,' she said, 'what your relations are with this young woman. It would be dishonest of me to say that I don't care, but you know I am broad-minded and I don't think you would find me lacking in understanding if' — Veronica lost herself for a moment; but not for long — 'if you have found it necessary to punish me for the unhappy ending to our last meeting. So far as I am concerned, this whole unfortunate episode could be forgotten.'

Veronica paused to let her words penetrate, and her eyes named Bertie and Charlie as the chief culprits in the 'unfortunate episode'.

'But,' she went on in a stronger voice, 'I must make one thing perfectly clear. If, after all you have said to me about your convictions, after marching to Alder-maston with me, after convincing me that you were a man endowed with a strong moral sense, you allow yourself to drift weakly back into the army as soon as they crook their fingers at you — then I am finished with you! Finished, once and for all.'

Henry looked back at her blankly, unable to help. He wanted to give her some personal reassurance — for they had after all been close, in a sense, at one time — but it could not be done. Veronica made one last appeal:

'I do understand what you're doing, Henry,' she said, in a softer voice than she had used before; 'I understand, and in a way I admire you for it. Your friend here is going back to the army, probably against his will, and you feel you can't refuse to go with him, it would be letting him down. I know you managed to stick together when you were in the army before, and I know how strong this kind of male loyalty is. I'm not really so stupid, or so lacking in human feeling, as I think you imagine. But there are greater loyalties than personal ones, you know. There is loyalty to an idea, for instance — not to mention loyalty to God. If we were married, I would expect you to put your ideals before your wife, if the interests of the two conflicted. And a friend who was any kind of real friend would expect you to do the same.'

Henry half expected Charlie to answer this, for the last words were directed at him. But Charlie was silent, sucking his empty pipe reflectively, his eyes on Henry. Bertie, too, seemed to be waiting for him to speak.

He swallowed, and stood up, finding now the same difficulty as Veronica had done in knowing what to do with his hands. 'I'm sorry, Veronica,' he said. 'It's no good. I'm not a pacifist, you know — not your kind. I never shall be. Whatever I did, it would never be for the reasons you would want me to do it. I've just got to do — what I've got to do. That's all. I'll write to you — from Catterick — as soon as I can, and try to explain. I'm not very good at . . .' — he made a gesture with his hands to include the whole situation — 'but it's no good, I'm afraid. I'm sorry. It's no good going on.'

'I see,' said Veronica quietly. 'Then I'd better go. If you change your mind — you know where I am. You may despair of me, Henry, but' — she gave a watery smile. 'I shall never despair of you. Goodbye.'

With Veronica's departure, Bertie was able to give way to the tears which she had been storing up. While Henry comforted her in his arms, Charlie, whistling unconcernedly, started to cook bacon and eggs on the electric ring. When her snuffling had ceased, Bertie withdrew to the bathroom for repairs.

'Nice girl,' said Charlie.

'Yes,' said Henry.

'More your type, I'd say.'

'I suppose so.'

'Hey, don't be like that,' said Charlie, alarmed. 'You know bloody well she is, don't you?'

'Well, of course,' said Henry. 'The trouble is — I feel such a heel.'

'Let's face it,' said Charlie. 'You *are* a heel.'

Bertie came in, her face shining.

'You aren't really engaged to that woman, are you, darling?' she asked.

'Of course not. Let's not talk about her now. I'll tell you the whole story one day.'

'I felt awful, arguing that you *ought* to go in the army, when it's the last thing in the world I want to happen!'

Henry noticed how much more relaxed they were together now that Veronica had gone; as if a real enemy had been removed from the camp. And yet, in an obscure way, he knew that he admired Veronica more than he admired Charlie, or himself. Bertie, he simply loved — how easily the word came to his mind! But Veronica — it seemed that she belonged to a different race, with which his own race could not communicate. They spoke different languages, would

never understand one another. He had to admire —
but, oh, the relief at being home again!

Charlie said, grinning: 'You've got a bit of explaining to do, old fruit.'

'So I have,' said Henry. 'Sit down, Bertie, I want
to tell you a story.'

As Henry had expected, when Bertie heard that he
was not in fact going back to the army, and his
reasons, and, parenthetically, Charlie's reasons, she
made an effortless *volte-face*.

'Oh, that's marvellous, darling! And you're so
right, people shouldn't go around killing each other,
it's bad for them. Golly Moses, I do think you're
clever, being able to think things out like that! I
never know *what* I think. And I've always wanted
to go to Wales.'

'Go to it, boy,' said Charlie, crouched devotedly
over the frying pan. 'Explain, explain.'

Henry went on explaining.

Chapter Eight

IF Brigadier McNeil ever got to know about the loss of that report, it would be curtains for Colchester. McNeil had never for a moment questioned Colchester's ice-cold courage, nor his rapier-sharp intelligence, but there had been a number of awkward occasions in the past when the Brig. had had cause to warn him that his unique virtues would all be to no avail if he failed to control his besetting sin — carelessness.

Colchester had done his level best to cultivate the 'security sense' proper to a secret agent, but with alarmingly little success. He recalled how Domenica, regarding him solemnly with her sad, lustrous brown eyes across the café table in Valetta, had told him: 'You have the Death-Wish, my Pedro! Believe me, I know it, I see it in your cool blue eyes. These lapses of yours that your Commandant complains of — they are not so strange, after all.' She had leaned towards him, her gaze mutely appealing, her low dress gaping open distractingly. 'Nothing is an accident, my Pedro! These things happen because you wish to die!'

Henry sighed, his body soft with longing for the sultry threat of Domenica's embraces. It was not difficult, on such an oppressive summer morning as this, isolated in the airless cell of his mosquito net,

to slide drowsily back into a re-creation of those first
magical days with Domenica in the hotel San Antonio
at Taormina, high above the turquoise heart of the
little bay, with the cicadas singing in the lemon groves
and the warm autumn sun touching their naked bodies
awake each magical, sparkling morning . . .

And yet, Henry was uncomfortably aware, there was
something wrong with his memories of Domenica.
She had changed in some subtle way, there was a new
softness in her eyes, a touch almost of shyness in her
love-talk. He had difficulty, now, in imagining the
new Domenica unstrapping from her brown thigh
the delicate, needle-sharp stiletto in its soft chamois-
leather sheath, and laying it on the pillow beside them
as they prepared to make love; and these nervous,
excited hands were surely not the same as those pur-
poseful ones that had coolly strangled the eunuch
with a silk stocking during the Caucasian escape?

Henry pushed these thoughts aside. He had to work
out what had happened to that report, and devise a
scene of bloody carnage from which Krossov, de-
feated, and Domenica, Wu Pin Chi and himself, vic-
torious, would all emerge alive, ready for further
adventures in the next book. It was now clear that
Krossov was also in Aden, and not only knew where
Colchester was staying but actually had access to his
room . . . for the time being, Krossov had the upper
hand, and Colchester was in extreme danger. This
danger, Henry decided, must be increased before it was
dispelled.

At this moment Henry experienced a curious and
very alarming sensation. It was just as if the foot of his

bed were being lifted very slowly but inexorably into the air. After a few moments of this odd delusion, Henry distinctly felt the bed rock slightly from side to side; and he then became aware that the sensation was not a delusion at all, for he was having to grip the sides of the bed with both hands to prevent himself from slipping down head-first through the mosquito net to the floor. His feet were now considerably higher than his head, and still rising.

As the curtains of the room were drawn, and the mosquito net nearly opaque, Henry could not see what was happening, but he was convinced that his whole bed was now suspended somewhere up in the air, halfway between floor and ceiling; and that if he got out of bed without the greatest care he was in for a very nasty fall indeed. Moving cautiously, he began trying to turn his body round so that his feet, instead of his head, should point towards the floor. This accomplished, he rested for a moment, his mind whirling with possibilities. It was then that he became conscious that there was someone else in the room: he could hear heavy breathing, the sort of muffled, difficult breathing of someone who does not want their presence to be detected. Krossov, of course. Henry's body became rigid with fear.

In the past, in the course of writing his Peter Colchester books, Henry had many times found himself devising intricately appalling predicaments for his hero, and had sometimes paused to wonder, gratefully, at his own ingenuity. His imagination had never found difficulty in 'thinking backwards' from effect to cause, and he had no inclination to enquire into the reasons men might have for perpetrating upon each other the terrible tortures which he believed to be the common-places of international espionage. Thus in this present crisis Henry's mind did not fruitlessly seek to discover *why* he should be ambushed in this manner, but instead ran feverishly along its accustomed rut: *what happens next*. Was there a trapdoor in the floor just beyond the head of his bed through which (had he been asleep) he would helplessly have slithered? And, if so, what lay below? A dungeon? The Bosphorus (no, not below Aden) . . . a pit of lions? And if, in a desperate bid, he were to leap blindly through the mosquito net and dive for the window, would his feet be im-paled on the six-inch spikes with which Krossov would surely have thought to have carpeted the floor?

Such wild imaginings occupied Henry's attention, of course, for a few seconds at the most; but were vivid enough to have set him sweating with fear. Dis-missing all thoughts of Krossov and Colchester from his mind, he sought for more rational explanations. Finding none, he realised that he would have to brave whatever dangers lay outside the little muslin tent which still enveloped him. The heavy breathing had stopped, and Henry was sure that he was now alone in the room. Cautiously, he lifted the skirt of the net and advanced one bare foot over the lower end of the bed.

To his surprise his foot at once met the floor, exactly where the floor ought to be. Henry pushed aside the net and stood up, looking around him sus-piciously. There was no-one to be seen. He walked around to the foot of the bed. All at once became

clear to him. A large pneumatic jack had been wheeled
into position under the frame and pumped up to a
height of about eighteen inches. The angle of bed
thus obtained was not great, although it had seemed
so to Henry while he was in a horizontal position.
Henry sighed, irritated with himself now for not at
once jumping to the right conclusion. In the distance
he could hear screams of hysterical childish laughter,
and knew that his cautious, wild-eyed emergence from
the mosquito net had been observed with lunatic
delight by Elwyn's three savage sons. Henry crossed
slowly to the window and drew back the curtains.

This daily ritual of curtain-drawing had become for
Henry, in the past seven days, an action of the utmost
significance. In his London flat he seldom looked out
of the window except to peer down inquisitively at
visitors who were ringing the outside bells of the
other flats in the building. If he did happen to glance
out he would always see the same toneless façade
facing him from the other side of the street, with
above it a neutral strip of light which he knew to be
the sky only because it was where the sky ought to be.

But here in Wales the view from his room was each
day uniquely new, never to be repeated. The elements
might remain the same, but they appeared always in
different combinations, accepting daily a different
emphasis. This morning the bright noon sun was
laying its accent across the flat sands of the estuary,
laid out with all its channels and pools and humps
like a yachtsman's map; and between Henry and the
glittering waters a thousand feet below him were
interposed shifting layers of heat which made the rocky

hillside seem insubstantial, and the misty blue mountains on the other side of the river no more than a
mariner's mirage.

The shallow valley, with its neatly cultivated fields
firmly walled off against the advancing tides of heather
and bracken on either side, sloped down from the
farmyard outside Henry's window and lost itself in a
scoop of scrub oak where the streams joined and the
richer farms began. Today it was a vessel full of thick,
sluggishly moving air; but when Henry opened the
casement he was grateful to find that a small cool
breeze was disturbing the ridge on which the farm-
house crouched. He knew, without thinking about it,
that on days like these when the heat hangs closely in
valleys and the distance dances, such unexpected
breezes heralded thunder and solid, drowning rain.
Sighing again — this time at some vague apprehension
that his life was a waste of such inherited knowledge
— Henry turned back into his room and regarded his
cantilevered bed. Then, still in his pyjamas, he
padded through to the kitchen where Mair was clean-
ing eggs and packing them away in papier-mâché
honey-combs, layer upon layer piled up on top of the
deep-freeze cabinet. As Henry came in Mair looked
up, smiling faintly She smiled most of the time, but
never very broadly, and it was impossible to tell
whether she approved or disapproved, was happy or
sad, calm or disturbed. Charlie said she had 'admirable poise', but to Henry her lack of openness was
frightening.

'Good afternoon, Harry,' she said.

'Go on, Mair, it's not that late!'

'It's nearly twelve.'

'Where's Elwyn?'

'He's gone up the cwm with Charlie, they're washing the yearlings today. They were up at six and had gathered the yearlings by nine. El was hoping you'd be up in time to gather the mountain, but he told me not to disturb you if you hadn't appeared.'

'He hadn't said anything to me,' said Henry. 'I've been doing some thinking.'

'Oh, yes?' said Mair absently. She always said this, in a voice which expressed deep interest, whenever she had ceased to listen to what was being said.

'Mair, come into my room for a moment, will you? I've got something to show you.' Mair followed Henry reluctantly towards his bedroom door, where he stood aside to let her enter first. 'Look,' he said, waving his hand towards the bed.

Mair looked, first at the bed, then at the jack, then at the mosquito net, and finally all round the room. Then she looked back at the bed.

'What did you do that for, Harry?' she asked. 'I should think it's most uncomfortable.'

'I didn't do it, you ass!' said Henry testily. He knew that Mair would not relish being called an ass, but he felt at odds with the world this morning. 'Your beastly children did it, while I was still in bed.'

'Which particular beastly child?'

'I don't know. I couldn't see. I told you, I was still in bed.'

'Couldn't you have hopped out and caught them at it?'

'No.' Henry thought for a moment, and then said:

'I didn't know it was happening until it had already happened.' This sounded a little odd, he knew. Mair raised one eyebrow.

'Well, what do you want me to do about it, Harry? You don't know who did it, and I can't very well punish them all, can I?'

'I suppose not,' said Henry, feeling uncomfortable and foolish.

'You'll just have to be more fierce with them, Harry. They wouldn't dare do a thing like that to Charlie, would they? Even if,' Mair added with her little smile, 'Charlie slept under a mosquito net too.'

'I just thought it might amuse you,' Henry muttered. He started to take off his pyjama jacket. 'I won't have any breakfast, Mair. I'll just get cleaned up and do a bit of work before lunch, if that's all right . . .'

Mair had already left the room; she was a little prudish, as Henry knew, and didn't really like seeing him in his pyjamas, let alone half out of them. 'It's nearly lunchtime now,' she called back over her shoulder. 'You'd better hurry.'

In fact the boys had already gobbled their meal and fled by the time Henry returned to the kitchen. Tad, Elwyn's father, who ate very little these days, had had a plate of soup on his knees, sitting in his chair outside the front door; whence, gazing down the valley with his bleached blue eyes, he could people the farms and homesteads with the figures of his youth. Henry ate alone, in silence, pretending to read the newspaper but in fact trying to sort out Colchester's predicament into a credible pattern. After lunch he made a cup of Nescafé, out of his own tin, while Mair made a pot of tea for herself and Tad. He carried his cup back to the bedroom, and sat at the table by the window, sipping coffee and reading through the dozen or so uninspired pages which he had written since his flight to Wales.

They were no good, that was quite clear. Something had gone wrong, and Henry couldn't understand it. Previous experience told him that at this stage in a book nothing *could* go wrong, it was simply a question of engineering an exciting, bloodthirsty final scene, tying off the loose ends, and setting Domenica and Colchester on the road to some romantic holiday resort. It ought all to be perfectly simple and straightforward — but it was not. He had come up against a block of a kind which he had never met before, and had no idea how to deal with it. For some reason the thought of writing that final scene of violence, instead of making him tingle with excitement, produced a faint but recognisable feeling of nausea.

His eyes wandered from the typewritten sheets, and he saw Tecwyn, the second son, flying across the fields below in pursuit of his 'pet' lamb, which had been reared by hand but was no longer tame. He could hear the other boys jeering and laughing. Down on the estuary one of the lobster boats was creeping seaward along the narrow river channel. The sky, though still cloudless, had become dull and heavy. Somewhere an aeroplane was interminably buzzing, seeming neither to get nearer nor further away, a sound which produced in Henry, for some reason, a feeling of restlessness which was almost unbearable.

The air was so still now that when a railway train shunted off some of its carriages down at Bont Newydd Junction, four miles away, the metallic clanking came through Henry's window like the sound of a harrow being dragged across stones in the next field.

Feeling oddly disturbed, as much by the atmosphere of the day as by the chaos of his own thoughts, Henry gave up and went out to the yard to sit beside Tad in the afternoon sun. Tad was a tiny, humorous man with a face like last year's chestnuts, cracked, creased, and dry. In his romantic youth Henry had thought of Tad as an Old Man of the Hills, full of some fundamental wisdom unattainable by townsfolk; and he had sat dutifully at Tad's feet, on just such heavy afternoons as this, waiting for the casual wisdom to flow. But he had found, after patiently sitting out two or three of these vigils, that Tad's conversation was restricted to quotations from the *Liverpool Daily Post*, and complaints about the economics of hill farming. Forty years of striding the mountains in all weathers had bred in Elwyn's father, it seemed, no conclusion more startling than that sheep didn't pay these days the way they used to. His early devotion, however, had its reward, for Tad liked him. Tad liked so few things and people that this was for the young Henry a most flattering accolade, despite Elwyn's jeers about 'the emptiness communing with the vacuum'.

'Ah, Harry,' the old man said, when he became aware that Henry had settled beside him, 'I was just thinking about you, sitting by yourself cooped up in there, working away with your head. That's all wrong on a day like this, in't?'

Tad spoke in English, a language which he handled better than many an Englishman of his own class, for he loved the sound of words even when they meant little to him. Henry, whose own parents had not been Welsh-speaking, for they came from the adulterated North Coast, had never been fluent in Welsh and had by now lost too much of it to carry on a prolonged conversation.

'Mind you,' went on Tad, 'don't think I don't respect brains. I always knew you was a proper scholar, you ask El. I was always saying to El, there, if only you had the brains of young Harry you'd be all right, boy. You'll do no good in life, I'd say, if you can't use your head, isn't it. But he wouldn't keep to his books, not El. He's just as stupid as ever he was. Look at today, now.'

'Today?'

'What's he doing, isn't it. Fancy washing on a day like this!'

'You think it's going to rain, then, Tadda?'

'There you are, you see. You've got it, you use your head. There's no point washing if you can't shear within two-three days, is it? It'll rain before midnight, and it'll rain for a week then. I told him, but he wouldn't listen, he's got no brains, hasn't Elwyn.'

Henry said nothing, for it had always seemed to him that Elwyn had a very good brain, that perverseness and laziness were Elwyn's faults, not stupidity. It was true that he disliked using his mind, but that was by choice: as a youth he had written more intelligent essays, better poetry, than anyone in the school.

'Couldn't Elwyn put the yearlings in the barn, Tadda, just for tonight?' Henry suggested. 'Then if it wasn't raining he could let them out to dry off, and shear on Tuesday as planned. There's just a chance it'll only be a quick storm.'

Tad puffed silently at his pipe, wearing that withdrawn expression which Henry had once taken for pendent wisdom. 'He *could*,' Tad said at length. 'He *could*. Mind you, I think when it comes, it'll stay. But you never know, with weather. There you are, Harry, isn't, that's what I mean, brains, you see.'

Tad continued to stare down the valley, apparently deep in thought. Then he said: 'Oh, it was a lovely fish I got out of the long pool below Pistyll-gwyn that time. We'd been courting, but I couldn't resist looking, and there it was, waiting for me. A lovely fish, clean run. Fourteen and a half pound. I give it to her Mam, and I've always regretted that. If I'd known she was going to go off with that Dafydd Graig-ddu, I'd never have give that fish to her Mam. It was a lovely fish. Seven sea-lice I took off it! Seven! Can't have been in the river a week.'

'How did you take it, Tad?' asked Henry, wanting to hear more. But Tad had come back now from that clear untarnished moment of joy when he had stood below the waterfall with the great fish jerking in his hands and the girl watching fearfully from between the trees.

'How would it be,' he said, 'if you was to walk up the cwm now and tell him I suggest he puts them in the barn tonight? Do you good, a walk in the sun, and I'm sure you've earned it, working hard with your head all morning like that, isn'it?'

Henry agreed that it would do him no harm, and went through to the kitchen to tell Mair what he was doing. Mair said 'Oh, yes?' in her special way, and went on loading the egg trays into their boxes. Henry took a shepherd's crook from the fireplace, pulled on a pair of nailed boots, and set off slowly along the banks of the stream that came down beside the farm-house. Walking uphill was hot work, and soon Henry was able to empty his mind of everything save the necessity for conserving effort; the only image that stayed with him was that of Tadda's salmon, beating the grass flat with its great tail on that wonderful evening forty years ago.

The stream had been dammed to deepen and widen a pool below a small waterfall. At the head of the pool, beside the fall, a slate platform had been built out from the bank over the water, where the mouth of a stone pen opened on to the stream. The pen was built like a funnel, the narrow end towards the water, so that the sheep, pressed down by the dogs from the broad end until they were packed tight from side to side, could stand no more than two abreast as they reached the exit. In this exit, when Henry arrived, stood Charlie, one ewe gripped between his knees, another held outwards towards the platform, its fore-legs clear of the ground. Elwyn, at the very edge of the platform, had just dropped a large ram into the deep end of the pool, and was watching it struggle clumsily towards the shallows at one side. As Henry clambered down the steep rocks at the side of the pen

Elwyn reached behind him for the ewe which Charlie was holding out, swung it up into the air in front of him and let it drop, mutely struggling, into the swirl of water below his feet. Both men were naked to the waist and dripping with sweat. The surface of the pool, which would have been translucent earlier in the day, was now covered in a brown, greasy scum; loose wool washed from the sheep had collected like sea-foam along the edges of the pool.

Elwyn turned back automatically for the next victim, saw Henry, and paused. He leaned back against the wall of the pen, wiping sweat from his eyes with the tips of his fingers. Then he looked up at Henry, grinning madly.

'Managed to get up in the end, did you, boy? Well done! You'd better sit down, you must be exhausted after your long walk, eh? Eh? Eh?'

'Ar, dry up,' said Henry, who was indeed feeling rather tired. 'Tad sent me up to say why don't you put them in the barn tonight, he's sure it's going to rain and you'll never have them dry for Tuesday if you leave them out. It seems a good idea to me.'

'It might to you, little pig,' said Elwyn, showing his teeth scornfully, 'but to me the suggestion smacks of advanced senile decay. It isn't going to rain, not before Tuesday, and if it does it'll last for a week, and a fat lot of good it'll do having the bloody animals in the barn then.'

'It'll rain tonight,' said Henry, and had the satisfaction of seeing Charlie nod in agreement. But neither were prepared to argue the point. They both knew that argument only served to drive Elwyn further and further away from anything recognisable as a fact into some dream-land of god-given knowledge where he was always and unchallengeably right.

'You'd do better,' Elwyn said, 'to stop yackering about things you don't understand and get in the pen there, give poor old Charlie a spell. He's nearly dead now, he's had all the substance sucked out of him by overmuch communion with the Blessed Virgin, he's all run to religious fat, it's a terrible thing to see.'

Charlie was not at all reluctant to let Henry take over. His job, handling two struggling animals at once without ever having the chance of even ten seconds' rest, was by far the more arduous of the two; and though he was strong and reasonably fit, it was years since he had done any physical work. Henry, of course, was in the same condition, but there were only about thirty animals left in the pen, where there must have been two hundred to start with. Nevertheless it was not long before his arms and fingers were screaming for relief. The sheep struggled wildly as soon as they saw the opening, the road to freedom, in front of them; and it was all Henry could do, with the fingers of both hands buried deeply in their fleeces, to hold them back until Elwyn was ready for them. The sweat streamed in rivulets down his face, into his eyes, into his mouth, he could taste it, rank and salt, on his tongue. Seven more to go, five more to go, three more, the last two . . .

'That's the lot,' he said at last, straightening slowly, watching the head of the last ewe reappear on the surface of the pool, wild-eyed and blowing wetly.

'The lot?' said Elwyn, turning, sounding surprised.
'No, look, there's one behind you.'

As Henry turned to look Elwyn gripped him by the
waist and swung him out over the pool. As he fell
Henry was able to clutch at Elwyn's belt, pulling him
off-balance. Elwyn teetered wildly on the brink for an
instant, and then fell forward just as Henry was sur-
facing, pushing him under again. When he came up
the second time Henry was able to clout Elwyn on
the side of the head with his fist, but it was a poor
revenge. The water was stinking with the dirty grease
from two hundred mountain sheep. Strands of filthy
wool were clinging to his hair and had stuck among
the sparse hairs on his chest. Elwyn, struggling to the
bank on the other side of the stream, was shouting
with delighted laughter. Henry laughed too, but he
was not particularly amused. Too many 'jokes' of this
kind had happened to him in the last week. Elwyn's
temperament demanded that not a day should go past
without something — anything — happening. This
ducking would make his day.

'Don't come near me, man,' said Charlie, grinning,
'you stink.'

Henry chose to wash in a pool twenty yards up-
stream. On his way back he passed Elwyn with averted
eyes, feeling foolish but unable to force out of himself
the expected jocularity. He was behaving oddly,
and knew it, for puppyish practical jokes had been the
accepted small-change of his relationship with Elwyn
for as long as he could remember, and it was part of
their schoolboy code to take them well. He felt now
as a fat man is supposed to feel, in whom there is a

thin man struggling to get out. Changes, he could sense, were taking place inside him, too radical for easy assimilation into the Harry Hughes that Elwyn knew.

'Well,' said Charlie, as Henry rejoined him, 'how's that for a wasted morning? You're right about the rain, it'll be here by midnight.'

'Don't you mind?'

'Mind? Good God, no! You've got to accept this sort of thing if you live with El. After all, he's paying me to work for him; it makes no odds to me whether it's a waste of time or not, does it?'

'It would to me,' said Henry.

That evening Henry and Charlie decided to go down the mountain for a drink. Charlie wanted to collect the newspapers, which he had not seen for a week; Henry simply wanted as much beer as he could comfortably hold. Both agreed to help with the milking so that Elwyn could go with them. As they sat back to back in the shippon, with their heads pressed into the warm smelly flanks of their respective cows and the milk ringing into the buckets, they could hear Elwyn singing the *Gwynedd Gwyn* in his beautiful clear tenor as he swilled out the dung on the other side of the stalls.

'You can't be angry with El for long, can you?' said Charlie.

'Who said I was angry?'

'Come off it. You've been like a bear with a sore head all day.'

'It isn't Elwyn I'm sore at, then. It's Harry bleeding Hughes. I make me puke.' Henry laughed, to take some of the solemnity out of this, but Charlie would not be deflected.

'What's up, lad? Conscience trouble? Or are you afraid the law will catch up with you?'

'I don't know,' said Henry. 'I just don't know. It isn't the law, I don't care tuppence about that. But something's wrong. I can't write.'

Charlie snorted, but said nothing. Without actually expressing disapproval of Henry's method of earning a living, Charlie had always refused to show any interest in the books themselves. From his occasional jokes about Colchester, Henry knew that Charlie must have read, or looked at, one or more of them, but he had never offered a comment; and in fact this omission was comment enough. Henry, far from resenting this attitude, was relieved by it, for it saved him from that occasional embarrassment which he had experienced when writing the first two books: what will Charlie think of this? But, since the subject had never been discussed, it had become, like Charlie's Catholicism, one of the empty rooms in the house of their friendship.

Later, as the three of them walked down through the sultry evening towards the village, in air that seemed to have turned green as sea-water as the storm came nearer, Henry asked: 'What if someone recognises us?'

'What if they do?' said Charlie. 'No-one but us knows that we were on the Reserve. We're taking a farming holiday at Ty Coch, to help with the shearing — remember? Unless you do something really daft, they won't give you a second look. It's better than if you were a complete stranger, in fact. People are curious about foreigners.'

Charlie had destroyed his recall papers, and had advised Henry to do the same. If there were enquiries when the Emergency was over, he would say that he had never received them — no-one could prove that he had, and there's no law to say you must read the newspapers. But Henry, for reasons he could not bring to light, had not destroyed his, but had instead concealed them between the pages of his manuscript.

'You two heroes,' said Elwyn, 'are both going to end in jug. I'm only interested in seeing how long it takes them to catch up with you.'

There was only a handful of customers in the bar of the Gwydyr Arms. The landlord handed Charlie a thick wad of newspapers, a week's accumulation of *The Guardian* and the *Daily Herald*. While Charlie skimmed through these, and Elwyn exchanged agricultural gossip with his neighbours, Henry managed to insinuate himself into a game of darts at the other end of the room, and was delighted to find that constant practice on his own dart-board had brought him to a pitch of near-equality with these Public Bar experts. It took him two games to get his eye in; but then, as the quality of his playing began to reveal itself, there were nudgings and whisperings among the other players and Henry felt himself increasing in stature; his lost Welsh accent reappeared, and forgotten Welsh phrases came spontaneously to his lips. When he at last lost two games in succession, and with them his position on the board, he retired happy, in some way more confident than he had felt for many days in his own identity.

Charlie, when Henry rejoined him, was looking

worried. He had pushed the newspapers aside and
was sprawling back on the bench, legs straddled, his
arms hooked over the low back-rest behind him. He
raised his eyebrows at Henry without smiling, and
said, as soon as Henry was seated: 'I don't like it,
Harry. I don't like it at all.'

'What don't you like?'

'This lot.' Charlie nodded towards the newspapers
on the bench beside him. 'The news. They're making
an unholy hash of the whole business. They'll find
themselves in a sticky position before long, if they
don't watch it.'

'I thought you said they hadn't got a chance anyway?'

'I don't mean the Castillians, you oaf,' said Charlie
patiently. 'I mean our lot. They've bungled the whole
thing, it could drag on for months now.'

Henry thought carefully for a moment; and then
asked: 'But I thought you were on the side of the
islanders, Charlie? Isn't that why you're here —
because you want them to win?'

Charlie suppressed a sigh. 'No, Harry,' he said.
'I'm here because I can't associate myself with our
Government's action — you don't imagine that what
I do could make a jot of difference to anyone but me?
The Castillians can't win because now we've started
it we can't afford to let them win. There was only
one point when we could have backed out gracefully,
and that was when the U.N. offered to put an arbitra-
tion force in. But it's too late for that now, it's gone
beyond anything a neutral force could control. What
galls me is that having made the wrong decision in the

first place, they haven't even the sense to carry it through properly. They've given the Castillians time to get organised, the Communists are sending every kind of help and getting a firmer grip on them every day. The whole situation's a hundred times more serious than it was, and it's going to get worse. It makes me feel sick.'

And he looked sick, and tired, as if he were personally responsible for what was happening in the Castillian Islands; like the woman from Woking who had lived out each minute of the Hungarian revolution in her own person, Charlie was suffering for others, and his suffering was real.

Elwyn was beside them now, having glanced quickly through the headlines of the papers with an expression of mounting enjoyment. 'Well, little pigs,' he said, 'feeling happier now?' Elwyn's only declared political position was that of a Welsh Nationalist, and he enjoyed needling each of them in turn. With Charlie, for whom he had most sympathy, his line was that if he really sympathised with the Castillians, he ought to be out there fighting for them, helping to counteract the Communist influence; with Henry, that if he used his imagination as a Welshman he would understand what it's like to be a member of a subject nation, suffering from the inadequacies of an economy not your own, supporting by taxes imperialist policies which are abhorrent to you, and having no say in affairs of state which affect your own future: and so would be unable to support a pacifist position.

Elwyn suddenly nudged Henry sharply in the ribs. 'Seen this, boy?' he asked, shaking a newspaper in front of Henry's face. 'It says here that three hundred and something recalled reservists have failed to report to their barracks and have been listed as deserters. That's you, mochyn bach. You're a bloody deserter, that's all you are.'

'I wish you wouldn't talk so loud,' said Henry.

'Three hundred,' said Charlie. 'That's not bad, not bad at all.'

'But it also says,' said Elwyn, no less loudly, 'that owing to the exceptional nature of the emergency it has been decided to grant an amnesty period, beginning on Saturday — that's today — and that deserters reporting to their depots during that period will have no proceedings taken against them. So there's still time to change your mind, Harry. You've been nervous as a kitten these last few days. Don't you think you'd be happier back in the nice warm arms of Mother Army?'

'No,' said Henry shortly, ashamed of the ridiculous surge of relief that went through him when he heard of the amnesty. He watched Charlie reach out for the newspaper and read the paragraph to himself, his lips tightening, his brow contracting. Henry longed for Charlie to make some strong, scornful remark; but Charlie said nothing. Elwyn peered into their faces sardonically.

'Well, boys,' he said, 'any takers? Charlie, now! Why not admit that you've been behaving like an emotional schoolboy and get back into line while there's still time? It's your last chance, you know. If you don't go back now, you've had it. It'll either be the glasshouse for you, or you'll be a farm labourer for the rest of your life, an outcast chained to a maniac called Elwyn Ellis, who'll keep you at subsistence level and wring the last ounce of work out of you under the threat of going to the cops. God, what a destiny, eh? Eh? Eh? Hadn't you better think again, boy? And you, Harry bach. Anyone can see you're being devoured by guilt, man! You've got a furtive look about you; if I was a bogey I'd arrest you on sight. You'll be a nervous wreck inside a fortnight. Is it worth it, boy? Why not jag it in while there's still time?'

'Ara, get stuffed,' said Henry, gathering their three empty tankards for a refill. Elwyn grinned wickedly, enjoying his role. 'Ask Owen Roberts there what he thinks about these deserters, Harry,' he called, as Henry approached the bar.

The only other customer at the bar was a tall, suspicious-looking man whom Henry had noticed before simply because nobody had spoken to him save to give a guarded greeting. He seemed to welcome Elwyn's invitation.

'Reading about these lads as haven't turned up at their barracks, is it?' he asked. 'Bloody scandalous, if you ask me. I'll tell you what I'd do with them. I'd have them shot, the lot of them. Oh, yes!'

'Isn't that a bit excessive?' said Henry mildly.

'Excessive, is it!' exclaimed Owen Roberts, seeming to swell visibly with indignation. 'I'll tell you, young sir, shooting is too good for them, by damn! Traitors, that's what they are. Communist dupes, the lot of them!'

Charlie was beside Henry now, to Henry's relief. 'I say, do you really think so, Mr. Roberts?' asked Charlie politely.

'Think what, young sir?'

'That all these boys who've failed to rejoin the army are Communist dupes?'

'Of course, of course. What else are they, may I ask? They've been got at, one way or another, you can believe me, sir.'

'How do you mean, "got at", Mr. Roberts?'

'Well now, you know the way these Communists work, sir. They're very clever, it's all done from the inside, isn't it? In-fil-tration, that's what it is. The Hidden Invaders.'

'You don't think,' asked Charlie, 'that some of these young men might have thought it out for themselves and decided that they couldn't have any part in this particular business, for moral reasons?'

'For *moral* reasons!' echoed Owen Roberts incredulously. 'Excuse me if I laugh. I can see you're a very intelligent young man, sir, but I don't think you can have been following the newspapers. It's as clear as daylight that this was all engineered by the Communists, nobody but a fool could argue with that, isn't it? And I'll tell you another thing. I'm a Welshman, now,' (Charlie, for Henry's benefit, had been speaking in careful English) 'but I fought against the Germans in one war, didn't I? And I'd have fought again if they'd have had me, only my job was too important, see? And I'll tell you this. I'd be out there fighting today if I was your age! Oh, yes! I'd show those black bastards a thing or two!'

At this point Henry found it politic to upset one of the new tankards of beer down Charlie's trousers, and make a great point of brushing him down; manœuvring him, incidentally, as far away from Owen Roberts as possible. Charlie was cool-headed and normally equable in argument, but he had a flash-point, Henry knew, which was easily reached when insults were offered to what Elwyn called 'our pigmented brethren'. Henry, usually not particularly quick-witted, had learned by experience to act with speed under such circumstances as these. Before Charlie knew what was happening, Henry had him sandwiched against Elwyn, leaving Owen Roberts triumphant and undisturbed at the bar.

'What are you doing, for Christ's sake!' muttered Charlie. 'Didn't you hear what that sod said? My God, isn't that typical, isn't that bloody shamefully typical? Lemme talk to him, lemme tell him about himself. Why don't you get out of the bloody way, you clumsy sod? Did you hear him? Listen, there's self-satisfied sadists like him all over the world, and they're the enemy, Harry, I tell you, *they're the enemy*! Take a good look. That's it! That's the enemy!'

Under Charlie's malevolent stare, Owen Roberts had become uncomfortable, aware that something was amiss beyond the tragedy of a spilled pint of beer. But, as Elwyn later explained, Owen Roberts was used to hard stares and cold shoulders. He was the local water bailiff, and at this time of year, when the salmon and sea-trout were coming up-river to spawn, he was everyone's enemy, for there were few locals who didn't consider they had an ancestral right to snatch a few fish for the larder while they were there for the taking. This explained, to Henry, Owen's isolation from the rest of the drinkers in the bar.

Owen Roberts finished his pint in one long swallow. 'Well, back to work, lads!' he exclaimed at large. 'Good night, young sirs,' he said, as he passed Henry and Charlie on the way out. 'Remember what I said. We've got to keep on top, isn'it. Otherwise we go down' — he pointed to the floor — 'we'll be dragged down to the same level as the savages! Oh yes!'

Henry and Elwyn held Charlie to his seat.

An hour later, insulated by alcohol against the weather, the three friends started back up the mountain in torrential rain. Their route lay initially through the swampy bottoms of some oak woods, where the rain spilled in irregular cupfuls from its catchments in the leaves above; then, as the valley narrowed, the path began to rise across slippery rocks, getting nearer and nearer to the little river, already swollen by the rain, which slipped by unseen in the narrow gorge it had cut for itself in the hillside. As the path rose the river too came up out of its depths, in a series of hidden waterfalls, until the two converged at the same level just where the struggling trees ended, for want of soil, and the bare mountainside began.

This was a spectacular place, even in daylight and sunshine. Two streams, one from each side of the spur on which Ty Coch stood, joined their waters at the very lip of a cliff, seventy feet above the level of the path where it emerged from the trees; and rushed down, not so much falling as slithering, into the long pool below. This was Pistyll-gwyn, the white waterfall, for even in summer when the streams were low the knobbly wall of the cliff broke the water to foam. Now, in near darkness, with the rain beating noisily on their shoulders and the growing wind streaming through the trees behind, the three young men stood for a moment in awe at the immense power of the white water thundering down towards them. Even Elwyn, to whom this was a familiar sight, hesitated, as always, at the edge of the woods.

Then to Henry's and Charlie's surprise, Elwyn said: 'Just stay where you are a moment, will you,' and strode forward purposefully towards the edge of the pool.

The bank on this side of the river had been cut away by countless years of wear to form a little bay; but then, at some time in the past, the river had changed the pattern of its flow — perhaps after a fall of rock — and had left this bay as a quiet, shallow backwater, untroubled by the writhing current of the main stream. It was here that Elwyn knelt down, pressed his face into the grass, and slid one arm, sleeve and all, down the bank and into the water. He seemed to stay motionless in this position for a very long time, his bottom in the air, his cheek against the ground; then suddenly he was convulsed with movement, there was a great splashing, audible even against the steady roar of the waterfall; and then he had the fish out on the grass in front of his face, it was beating the ground with its tail while Elwyn used his other hand to try to get it under control. Another convulsive movement, and Elwyn was bodily on top of the fish, both hands beneath him: and thus, for several seconds, he lay, quite still.

'Breaking its neck,' said Charlie, who had been poaching before. Henry wanted to run forward and help, but Charlie, with a hand on his elbow, held him back. 'Let him be,' he said, 'don't spoil it for him.'

When he tried to reconstruct the scene later, it seemed to Henry that the enormous figure of Owen Roberts had simply materialised out of the spume at the foot of the waterfall. At one moment there had been only Elwyn's recumbent figure on the bank, locked in motionless combat with his fish; at the next there was this giant of a man — only later identified to Henry as the water-bailiff — towering above him. In one hand was a large torch, unlit; in the other a heavy stick, raised as if to strike. The man shouted something in Welsh, but Elwyn did not move. He lay as if dead.

Charlie pulled Henry back a few steps into the shadow of the trees, whispering urgently: 'Come back! Back! Back! If I push you, rush him. Don't let him see your face. Don't speak in English, whatever you do. Keep near me . . .'

But in the event these exhortations proved unnecessary. Henry didn't see exactly what happened. He was aware only that Elwyn rolled suddenly sideways and stood up, the fish still hanging from one hand; and that as he did so the tall man stumbled, twisting violently, and fell backwards with a cry into the shallow water of the little bay. Then Elwyn was loping past them, not seeing them, down into the safety of the woods.

Charlie drew Henry a few yards off the path, and they crouched together behind a blackthorn bush while Owen Roberts clambered, dripping and cursing, out of the stream. It took him some time, in the growing darkness, to find his stick; longer to find his torch. Presumably knowing it to be hopeless, he made no effort to hurry off in search of Elwyn. He made rudimentary efforts to wring out the loose flaps of his clothing; searched the ground with his torch for possible clues to the identity of the poacher; flashed the beam, in a casual way, into one or two dark corners — dutifully, Henry thought, rather than hopefully — and then set off, squelching, down the path.

Elwyn, having climbed steeply up through the woods and back along the top of the ridge, while Henry and Charlie were still hiding behind their blackthorn, was already at Ty Coch when they arrived. The salmon, a male fish of about six pounds, in good condition, was in the refrigerator. Mair had gone to bed but Elwyn, his wet clothes steaming in front of the kitchen stove, was waiting up in jubilant humour to share his triumph with his friends.

During the next ten minutes Elwyn and Charlie reconstructed the whole episode, down to the smallest detail, from start to finish, at times so convulsed with laughter that they were almost incapable of speech. Henry sat quiet, occasionally laughing with them, putting in a question or a minor contribution to the saga, not isolated from them but knowing himself to have reserves about the incident which they did not share.

'When I saw who it was,' said Charlie, 'I nearly

jumped him. Typical of the fascist mentality, getting a job like that. If I wasn't on the run already I'd have gone and pushed him back in again. It's wonderful how the shits of the world manage to *label* themselves as shits for all to see.'

'Like the bloody bogies,' said Elwyn, 'sadists to a man.'

'Quite.'

Somehow Henry couldn't quite see life in these terms. He knew better than to argue, and supposed merely that he was not intelligent enough to appreciate the ideological subtleties which his friends seemed by their remarks to be suggesting. He had taken no particular dislike to Owen Roberts, though he disapproved of the man's views. He saw him simply as a rather stupid man, with attitudes common to his generation, who happened to be in a job which made him unpopular among the anarchically-minded.

'Don't tell Tad about Nowie Roberts, boys,' said Elwyn, as they went off to bed. 'Tad's a law-abiding man.'

'Damned young fool,' was Tad's comment in the morning, when he was shown the fish. 'That Owen Roberts is going to catch you one of these nights, Elwyn bach. Twenty pounds for a first offence, they tell me.'

He examined the salmon scornfully.

' 'Tisn't even a decent size fish, man diawl!'

Chapter Nine

As Tad pointed out, with satisfaction, he had said it would rain for a week, once it started, and it did. The storm which had been building up on Saturday evening, when Elwyn took the salmon, reached a crescendo of fury in the early hours of the following morning, rousing Henry from his sleep and making the heifers in the shippon which adjoined his room rattle their chains in unease. By midday the wind had dropped and the thunder had retreated far into the mountains; but the rain continued to fall, quietly, solidly, from a sky of unbroken grey. It was a sky which held out no hope of reprieve: the clouds were inexhaustible, the rain had a peculiarly vindictive quality, as if implacably resolved to wash the earth clean of all such sins as laughter, joy, warmth, dryness.

Outside Henry's window the sheep stood motionless, tails to wind, occasionally shaking themselves like dogs when the weight of their waterlogged wool became oppressive; otherwise simply enduring. A few yards away there was shelter, but they did not seek it. They stood like the petrified families of Pompeii, frozen in the positions in which this cataclysmic downpour had discovered them.

Elwyn, grimly inventing a series of unnecessary tasks outside, took pleasure in coming to stand, mud-

splashed and dripping, in the centre of the warm
kitchen: standing there with his arms held a little way
away from his body and his head bent slightly, so that
the water could drip off his cap and finger-tips, sardonically regarding his two friends while a little pool
of water collected round his feet; and would then
shake himself, and plunge once more out into the
rain, having said nothing but having succeeded nevertheless in making everyone in the kitchen feel slightly
uncomfortable.

The children, confined to the house for the best
part of each day, rapidly became impossible little
demons, constantly fighting, complaining, shouting
and daily surpassing themselves in the ingenuity of
the tortures which they devised for Henry; until
Henry was at length forced to make Mair search for
the key for his bedroom door. Mair, whose attitude
to the warfare between her children and her guest was
entirely impartial, clearly thought less of Henry for
this admission of defeat. She found the key, but
regarded his afternoon-long struggle to make the lock
work with tolerant amusement, offering neither help
nor encouragement. It was almost, Henry felt, as if
she looked upon these defensive measures of his as an
unwarranted restriction placed upon her children's
field of operations.

Every morning Charlie dressed himself up in oil-
skins, sou'wester, and gumboots, borrowed one of
Elwyn's crooks, and plodded stolidly through the rain
down to the village, to collect his newspapers. The
journey took three-quarters of an hour on the way
down, an hour and a quarter on the way back. Charlie

timed his walks so that he could sit alone each morning in the deserted bar of the Gwydyr Arms and sip a glass of Guinness while he read the most important sections of the newspapers. His journey occupied the major part of every forenoon, but since there was little farm-work that could be accomplished while the rain continued Elwyn did not object. It would have made no difference if he had. Charlie was obsessed by the news from the Castillian Islands, he could think of nothing else; daily he became more abstracted, the twin lines between his eyebrows became deeper, his hooded brown eyes seldom opened up for laughter. Mair was not a person given to betraying likes and dislikes, her thin smile rested with equal ambiguity on friend and enemy alike; yet it was possible to detect, in her tender, unquestioning tolerance of Charlie's silent mood, an unusual degree of approval. Mair liked people to be serious. Charlie was serious.

In his own way, Henry was now serious too. He was also happy. His happiness dated from the day he had received a letter from Bertie. The letter read:

'Darling Henry,

'Or shall I call you Harry, I think so, yes. Its awful here without you — how long is this going to go on — there haven't been any letters to forward. Dont think I dont understand why you have to do it this way but its awful for me without you because I love you. Vernon has been. I went down to the Denmark (didn't spend money its okay) and there he was and came back to see if I was comfy. Couldnt think why he shouldnt, hope I havent done wrong.

He was very nice and give me a bottle of gin — most of it still left — keep hoping you will walk in thru the door one day — and said I was a lucky girl he quite fancied you himself!!!! Well so do I!!! Shameless, that's me! Do write and say you will come back soon or can I come there? I got your cheque, havent cashed it yet, did some modeling at Slade and earned £3–3 aren't I clever.

'Sorry about awful letter but I do love you so there!!!

'Believe me yours truly,

'Berty.'

It was the misprint that went to Henry's heart: 'Shamless, that's me!' A heaven of human honesty opened before him, like that door to the perfect garden, an image from his childhood which he could never forget.

But it was not so much Bertie's letter that had made him happy, as something that had happened to his work. He had had a vision. It was quite extraordinary, something that had never happened to him before. Suddenly, while he was mulling over, in a dissatisfied way, the pattern of action which he had to work through in order to wind up this book, he had 'seen' Domenica, as he had never seen her before. Somewhere, somehow, Domenica had undergone a change so startling that Henry, thinking of her, was almost blinded by the beauty of his own creation. Not only was her nature beautiful, but her function was beautiful too: it had meaning. From being the ruthless, if sensual, *agent provocateur*, Colchester's third arm in his perpetual struggle with Krossov and the forces of International Communism; poisoner, strangler, member of harems, seducer of diplomats, the emotionless initiator of *affaires* which could only end in death for her lovers, she had become the messenger of mankind's salvation, the voice of warm reason, the shameless envoy of love. Domenica, in fact, had had a vision, and now had a mission: to wean Colchester from the cult of violence, make him a Good Man.

This revelation of Purpose was to Henry an experience of almost religious intensity. Except for mealtimes he kept to his room, the door locked, weaving into the completed part of his manuscript this transmogrified Domenica; making notes, shifting emphases; and, with a sensation not far short of acute stage-fright, draughting those new chapters in which Domenica swept down, like Gabriel's fiery sword, to exorcise the evil from Colchester's nature.

Several times during the week Charlie made attempts to start a political conversation, but Henry could not be drawn. Elwyn observed with sardonic amusement the silent struggle which went on in the kitchen at meal-times, with Charlie manœuvring for an opening, Henry stonewalling, apparently oblivious to the fury which was building up in his friend. As soon as he decently could Henry would slip away, smiling his thanks and apologies to Mair, too deeply involved in his imaginary world to know that he had given offence in the real one.

It was on Friday, almost a week after the episode with the fish, that a breach in Henry's defences was finally effected, and then not by Charlie but by Elwyn.

That morning, returning from the village with his papers, Charlie knocked loudly and impatiently on the panels of Henry's locked door. Reluctantly, Henry dragged himself from his desk, unlocked the door and opened it a few inches, peering out irritably through the crack. Charlie stood there, newspapers in hand, with the water streaming off his oilskin and his hair plastered down over his forehead, making his face appear more than ever like a badly battered piece of stone.

'Come into the kitchen, Harry,' he said abruptly. 'I want to show you something.'

'I can't come now, Charlie, I'm right in the middle of something — something absolutely *vital*!'

'It'll wait. This is important, Harry. Important for both of us.'

Henry closed the door another inch. 'I'm sorry,' he said firmly, 'I can't possibly come just now. I'll be out for lunch, you can tell me then.'

But Henry might have wavered; if Charlie had given an inch of understanding, Henry would have given a mile of sacrifice. But Charlie's face had set into bleak lines. 'You can't hide for ever, you know,' he said. 'You'll have to stop masturbating and start growing up one day.' He turned away abruptly, starting to shrug himself out of his oilskin as he went down the passage to the kitchen. Henry closed the door slowly, but left it unlocked. He crossed to the typewriter, sat down, and started to pummel his forehead with both hands. What did 'important' mean? To Charlie it obviously meant some startling development in the Castillian Islands. But this could not be 'important' to Henry. Whatever had happened, no political or military situation could force him to go and kill people. His decision was not complicated, like Charlie's, by difficult moral considerations. What was 'important', then, for him? To do what he was doing as well as possible; to avoid damaging other people's lives; to be independent, so that he could live according to his own values and not according to those of his masters . . . it didn't sound much, but these, Henry knew, were the 'important' things for him; and even these simple standards were not easy to keep. His independence was qualified by the fact that he was in debt, both to Charlie and to Elwyn; and it seemed that, by allowing his estrangement from Charlie to grow, he had tilled a field for bitterness. Sighing, he returned to his work. That at least retained its new-found virtue.

He went down to the kitchen for lunch expecting to be met with an attack, but nothing happened. Charlie didn't even look up from his newspaper when Henry sat down at the table. Elwyn, though, gave him a friendly grin. 'Going well?' he asked.

'Last lap,' said Henry, gratefully. 'Just coming up to the last fence.'

'Good work, boy. I'm going to read this one, I've got a personal interest in it. Is it good?'

'It's going to be the only one worth reading.'

'Well done, little pig,' said Elwyn, grinning.

Henry was glad to have had a chance to say this in front of Charlie; it somehow lessened his guilt.

When lunch was finished Elwyn said: 'Could you two boys spare me half an hour's work now? I won't

keep you long, there's just something I want to sort
out in the barn. Charlie?'

Charlie nodded. Henry, feeling warm towards
Elwyn for having shown an interest in his book, agreed
eagerly, and Elwyn led them in a dash through the
rain, across the yard to the barn. This building was
warm and dry, built solidly like the house of local
stone and slate. There was a pile of last year's hay
at one end; a harrow and a broken-down Jeep at the
other; and nothing else.

'Neutral ground,' said Elwyn, shaking himself like
a dog. 'Sit down, boys, I've got a treat for you.'

'What's this?' asked Charlie. 'What do you want
us to do?'

'Just sit, that's all,' said Elwyn. He crossed to the
Jeep and came back holding a flagon of cider, a half
bottle of gin, and three cups. 'A little tipple,' he said,
'gin and cider, mother's ruin, make you better.' He
started to pour the drinks.

'What are you up to, Elwyn?' said Charlie. 'I thought
you wanted us to do some work?'

'So I do. Noddle work. A bit of sorting out. Here
you are. Iechyd da pob un.'

'Twll din pob Saes.'

Lying side by side on the hay, they drank in silence
for some minutes. Elwyn was in no hurry, he was
enjoying himself, but Henry was restless. 'Look here,
El,' he said at length, 'if you really haven't anything for
us to do, do you mind if I go back? I've got work to do.'

'Yes, I do mind,' said Elwyn.

'The dedicated artist wants to be alone with his
creation,' said Charlie. 'Ha bloody ha.'

Henry was shocked to hear the bitterness in Charlie's voice. Neither of them had ever spoken to the other in such tones before.

'Well, and why not?' demanded Elwyn. 'It's better than mooning about the place in a bad temper all day, like some I could name. The boy's got a job to do, money to earn — that's fair enough, isn't it? Still, Harry, I want you here for a while yet, you've got some talking to do. I'm fed up with watching you two glaring at each other; a couple more days like this and you'll be tearing each other's throats out, and I won't have it. I like a quiet life, man diawl.'

'You're wasting your time,' said Charlie. 'You can't talk to him, he's too wrapped up in his bloody masterpiece. I've chucked my hand in, I'm not going to try again. Let it ride, El. What does it matter to you, anyway?'

'It matters,' said Elwyn, gazing into his cup.

'I've been trying to talk to him all week, but it's like talking to the wall. Didn't I come to your door this morning, Harry, and get sent away with a flea in my ear?'

'I didn't send you away with a flea in your ear, Charlie. You came at a bad moment. All I asked was for you to wait until lunch-time. I was right in the middle of something difficult, something important — to me, anyway — and you wanted me to start thinking about something quite different. I couldn't do it.'

'That sounds reasonable,' said Elwyn judiciously. 'You can't expect the man to break off in the middle, just when things are coming to the boil.'

Charlie jumped to his feet and stood in front of them, baring his teeth at each in turn. 'Look,' he said, 'Harry isn't blind. He can't imagine I've been splashing down to get the papers just for fun. He must have known that when I said it was important, I wasn't pulling his leg.' He turned appealingly to Henry. 'I don't understand you, Harry, honestly I don't. You *were* serious about this, you must have been, you're not the sort to put yourself outside the law just for a lark. But you don't seem to give a damn now. You've hidden yourself away in there, scribbling at your wretched little spy stories, as if you're terrified of knowing anything about anything. You haven't looked at a paper all week. Don't you *care* what's happening, doesn't it make an atom of difference to you one way or another?'

'No,' said Henry.

'I don't see why it should,' said Elwyn. 'He's refusing to fight because he's got moral scruples against killing, not this particular lot of killing. He'd feel the same if it was a just war.'

'Not moral scruples,' said Henry. 'I just can't live with it, that's all. One was enough.'

'But *would* he feel the same if it was a just war, though?' asked Charlie. 'That's what I can't believe. I mean, if he feels the war *ought* to be fought, surely it's just moral cowardice to keep out of it because he doesn't like it? You don't think I like the idea of killing people, do you?'

'Why bring all this up now?' asked Henry wearily. 'We've been through it all before, you know you can't budge me.'

'I'll tell you why, boy. This amnesty for deserters

ends tomorrow. And I'm leaving for Catterick in the morning.'

Elwyn seemed not in the least surprised; but to Henry the news exploded like a bomb which had lain undetected beneath his feet for days. He realised at once that this was something he ought to have known was going to happen; but this did not lessen the impact of the blow. For it was a blow. Charlie's presence at Ty Coch had made it all too easy for Henry to accept his own.

'I had an idea you were thinking that way,' said Elwyn. 'But why, Charlie? You didn't come here just for a holiday, either. You know what I think about it, you know I agreed with you, nothing on earth would make me fight the Castillians. Why have you changed your mind?'

'I haven't, really,' said Charlie, after a long pause. 'I still think it was despicable, the way we strong-armed our way in when it wasn't necessary, and overthrew an elected government like that. But the whole situation has changed in the past fortnight. You've seen the papers, El. I don't know how much you've read of them, but you must have gathered that the Communists have got complete control of the resistance now. It's a complete gift to the Russians, of course, since half the western countries and all the eastern ones think the same way as we do about the original action. They're parachuting in supplies and military experts, it's turned into a full-scale little war. The trouble is, it isn't between us and the Castillians any more — it's between us and the Communists.'

'Perhaps,' said Henry, 'they want a Communist government?'

'Don't be so bloody daft, man!' said Charlie angrily.

'You're doing a lot of assuming, aren't you?' said Elwyn. 'It's one thing to control a scattered resistance army, but quite another to take control of a Government, assuming we ever let them have one again.'

'Oh, grow up, El, for Pete's sake!' exclaimed Charlie. 'Don't you bloody liberal dreamers ever learn from experience? How many more countries have got to become Communist before you realise that when these boys talk about World Communism they aren't joking? You were just the same with the fascists. You go on hoping to reform them with patience and love, and they go on laughing up their sleeves and doing exactly what they want. When was anyone ever reformed by example, can you tell me that?'

'Bang goes Christianity,' said Elwyn.

'Bollocks! Christianity was and is spread by evangelism, not by example.'

'Dangerous things, faiths,' said Elwyn.

'Dangerous when they're evil, yes. I believe Communism is evil, and I believe that if we don't squash the Castillians now their next government will be a Communist one. While we're all fiddling about with methods of saving our face and trying to do the right thing all round they'll be in there and the thing's over, bang, and you can whistle for freedom then.'

'I wonder,' Henry said, 'if the Castillians are all that worried about freedom? I mean, the ordinary native islander who doesn't really know the difference between one sort of government and another? I bet all he wants is to be left alone to cut his cane and put his nets out — or whatever it is they do there — and get on with the important things, like making love, and singing, and bringing up the children. Why can't people leave each other alone? I'm not sure I wouldn't rather have World Communism than have this perpetual fighting going on all over the place, and everyone living in an atmosphere of constant fear . . . Oh, hell, I don't know, Charlie, I'm hopeless at politics, you know that, but it all seems so bloody senseless to me, it hasn't got anything to do with *living*!'

'Charlie's a Catholic, Harry,' said Elwyn, 'you've forgotten that. He's pledged to fight dialectical materialism.'

'Then he's the sort who make wars!' cried Henry. 'Anyone who's prepared to kill in order to protect a faith, can't have a faith worth protecting!' He came up short, feeling that by accident he had stumbled upon a truth. But he couldn't consolidate it. 'All most people want is to be left in peace,' he added weakly.

'And you imagine the Communists are going to leave them in peace, man?' Charlie stood like a washer-woman in the middle of the barn, hands on hips, elbows jutting forward aggressively. 'It's innocents like you who're the real danger, you know that? You blunder along with your eyes shut, hoping everything's going to be all right as long as you don't do any harm, as long as you keep your own hands clean. If you were an intellectual, you'd call yourself a Liberal Humanist, and pretend that meant you actually believed in something. But you don't. You just don't want to be bothered, that's all. I tell you, boy, liberal humanism

makes me puke, it's the wettest moral position humanity's ever invented, just an excuse for looking smug
and doing bugger-all. A lot of mish-mash. You talk
about leaving people in peace in one breath, and then
about preferring World Communism to the daily
struggle against it in the next. But the whole structure
of Communism is based on the idea that people ought
not to be left in peace. It wants to dictate what sort
of work they should do, how much they should earn,
what they should learn, what they should believe. It
wants to organise every last detail of people's lives —
that's not leaving them in peace, is it? Leaving religion
out of it, I still say there's something in human beings
which won't tolerate restrictions on what they're to
believe. People will put up with a lot, I know, to avoid
trouble. They'll let themselves be regimented and
bullied and half-starved. But take away from them the
right to believe in what they want to believe, and to
say that that's what they believe, and sooner or later
they'll get up and cut your throat. You'll never have
peace where you haven't got freedom — I know it's a
cliché, but it happens to be true. And if you think
peace is going to come because the majority of people
want it, you're stupider than I thought. It's no good,
Harry, you can't opt out of the bunfight because you
personally don't want a bun. You've got your bun,
but what about the millions who haven't? You live in
the world, you're a member of a community that has
certain ideals from which you benefit. And you ought
to be prepared to fight for them.'

'You didn't think that at first,' said Henry, 'and the
situation hasn't changed for me.'

'All right. I was wrong. I admit it. I was blinded by my own feelings about the British action, and your refusing to go seemed to be a different face of the same coin. I see now that it wasn't. Still, you wouldn't have gone, would you, even if you hadn't got this thing against killing?'

'Not if you'd got hold of me in time. You're a bit of a moral bully, you know.'

'I have to be, with you. If you won't think for yourself, I have to think for you.'

'Of course. Like the Communists, you mean?'

'No, not like the Communists, because I haven't any power over your actions in the end. You'll go your own pig-headed way whatever I say, unless I can convince you I'm right. That's what freedom means, Harry. I'm going to fight to preserve your right to disagree with me. That doesn't stop me from wishing you agreed. It's not going to be fun, anyway, but it would be a damn sight easier if you were with me. What about it, Harry?'

'Bunch of traitors,' growled Elwyn. 'What about my shearing?'

'Bugger your shearing,' said Charlie, looking at Henry.

Henry looked at the hay between his feet. His head swam with the unfamiliar effort of concentrating on all these intangible ideas which Charlie handled with such casual ease. He had to struggle to convince himself that these were 'real' issues, with a meaning for 'real' people. But somehow he couldn't *see* these people, couldn't imagine their figures and faces and minds — Castillians, Communists, Whitehall diplomats, Pentagon planners — Henry could not cloak them in the warm flesh that would give meaning to their actions, and to his own in relation to them.

He ought never, he thought angrily, to have got out of line in the first place: it wasn't allowed for people like him. The column went on marching blindly, happily, to catastrophe, but even the people who could see this still insisted that you should stay in step unless you could give good consistent reasons for getting out. It wasn't enough just to 'know', as Henry thought he knew, that the whole thing was a circus of lunatics, intellectuals like Charlie wouldn't allow it, they wanted to protect their prerogative for moral action by restricting it to people who could explain themselves in the correct abstract terms.

He began to feel very angry.

'All right,' he said at last, 'go and get on with your killing, but leave me out, leave me alone. I'm tired of being bullied into agreeing with ideas I don't understand. I had two years of it from Veronica and I'm fed up with it. I don't spend my time telling you what you ought to think, do I? You're a Christian, Charlie. I'd have thought one of the most forceful instructions your saviour ever gave you was to turn the other cheek, but it's not my business to interpret your religion for you, I'm prepared to let you have your cake and eat it if that's what you want. I don't want to live under Communism. But if it's a choice between that and taking the life of some poor boob who probably has no more idea what he's doing than I have, I'll opt for the Communism and see what I can make of it. Just leave it there, can't you?'

But Charlie could not leave it there. His face had become pale and tense, and the fingers which he ran through his hair were trembling slightly. 'My saviour, as you call him,' he said quietly, 'told me I'd have to fight for my faith. We've been fighting for it for two thousand years, and we've only nibbled at the edge of the world yet. Where do you think Christianity would be now if it had turned the other cheek? Dead as a Dodo, boy! You'd probably be dead yourself if we'd gone on turning the other cheek in 1939 the way we did in 1938, and 1936 . . . You know what, Harry? It's people like you, with your delicate little consciences, that are going to destroy the world. And when it's all going up in flames you'll be sitting back and congratulating yourselves that at least it wasn't *your* fault — when in fact you and people like you are as culpable as the wickedest politician that ever walked. Why? Because you did nothing! It's all very well for you to say that all you want is to be left alone, but the fact is if *I* leave you alone — if I behave like you and leave everyone alone, and everyone in the Western world decides to leave everyone else alone — what do you think is going to happen? You don't imagine the Communists are going to leave you alone, do you? Harry, you've got to make up your mind, it's no good just sitting around and complaining that it's unfair of people to want you to think, you've bloody well *got* to think, now, you've got to stop pretending that nothing's happening, you've got to realise that things don't just *happen* in this world, they happen because people make them happen, and people means *you*, Harry. This isn't just a question of whether or not you'd rather live under the Communists than kill someone; it's a question of whether you'd rather kill someone than see the world devastated by H-bombs.'

'I don't follow you,' said Henry.

'I'm frightened,' said Charlie. 'I've had plenty of time to think in the past fortnight, and what I've thought about frightens me. And you know what frightens me most of all? The fact that previously I *haven't* been frightened! I've been too busy, or too lazy, or too happy to think. But now I've done some thinking, and I can see people all over the world, people like us, simply refusing to think because the thing they've got to think about is too big and too fearful to fit in with their daily lives. But we've got to think, Harry, we've got to know what we're doing, or we shall all perish. You know what I'm talking about, don't you?'

'I seem to remember,' said Elwyn, 'that Harry marched from Aldermaston two years running. He's one up on both of us on this wicket.'

'Granted,' said Charlie, smiling at last. 'Good for him, even if he didn't know why he was there — that right, Harry?'

'Dead right,' said Henry.

'And if I'm not still in the army, or dead, next year, I'll be marching myself. Not because I think you'll ever achieve anything, politically, that way, or even that it's desirable that you should, but because it may prise a few ostrich heads out of the sand. I'll sit in Whitehall, too, if it comes to that — anything, anything you like, just so people start thinking about the whole bloody business. But just now I've got something more immediate to do. Every time a little country like Syria, or Cuba, or the Castillians, is allowed to move quietly into the Communist orbit, the world moves a step nearer to self-destruction — do you realise that? Unless we can contain them, unless we can hold them back and make them believe that they're not going to win, someone, sooner or later, is going to drop that bomb. Either we'll drop it, because the Communists have crept on so far that we've left it too late to stop them any other way; or they'll drop it, because they've got away with so much they reckon they can get away with the last throw, too. The only hope, at the moment, is to keep the balance roughly the way it is, and to go on keeping it until someone finds a way of banishing these bloody bombs for ever. Or until we get some sort of World Government, though God knows how that's going to come about. But there's one thing you can't be in the world as it is, Harry, and that's a pacifist. There just isn't time for it to work.'

Charlie rested his case. Elwyn had lumbered to his feet, and now stood waiting to see if Henry had anything more to say. But Henry, buffeted by this cataract of words, could not, to save his life, have plucked from the whirlpool of his thoughts one single coherent speech. He shook his head at Elwyn, and turned his face to the hay.

'All right, Charlie,' said Elwyn, 'now you listen to me for a minute. I'll tell you something. Good news. I agree with you. You've put it in a nutshell the size of the *Queen Mary*. Cut down to size, you're saying

that you can't any longer find a moral reason for resisting your recall, so you're going. Okay. I admire
your honesty. Now I'll tell you something else. More
good news. I agree with Harry too. Not that he's
said anything, but we know what he thinks better
than he does. He knows that killing people is not
for him. Get it into your noddle, Charlie, that you
and Harry aren't the same person. What's right for
you isn't necessarily right for him . . .'

'Now, look, Elwyn,' burst out Charlie, 'that isn't
the point at all . . .'

'Shut up! Stop yacking! You've been bullying
Harry for half an hour, now give over. Listen! You
believe that Jesus Christ is the Son of God. I don't.
I think your religion's a lot of mystical hooey. But
I'm not going to argue with you about it because I
know that without it you'd go mad. You'll pretend
to me that you have intellectual reasons for believing
in God. Bollocks! You believe in him because you've
got to believe, you couldn't live without it. Same
with Harry. He's seen what happens when he kills
a man, he knows what happens to himself. If you like,
he had a religious experience, and it's left him with a
conviction as unshakeable as yours. If he goes against
that, he'll do such damage to himself as will one day
do far more harm in the world than he could do good
by his fighting. You be moral in your way, Charlie,
and let Harry be moral in his.'

'Elwyn,' said Charlie, 'you talk a lot of crap.
Doesn't he talk a lot of crap, Harry?'

'I don't know,' said Henry, out of a misery he could
not begin to fathom. 'I don't know what he's talking

about. I only know I'd like better than anything else to be coming with you tomorrow. But I can't.'

'Why?' cried Charlie. 'For Christ's sake, why? Just give me a reason that'll hold water for two seconds!'

'I can't. I don't know. I can't explain.

'I'm sorry,' Henry added, as he walked past them, out into the rain.

'Oaf!' said Elwyn to Charlie.

'You're wet,' said Charlie to Elwyn. 'Both of you. Wetter than this bloody mountain. Wetter than the Church of England. Wetter than the Liberal Party. Wet, wet, wet!'

Chapter Ten

WHEN Henry returned to the farmhouse after his long, damp walk across the mountains, his mind was no clearer than it had been when he had shambled out of the barn three hours before. He was soaked to the skin, and physically exhausted; and yet, in some way, he felt very much better, both in mind and body, than he had done for days. He felt clean. Nothing that Charlie might recognise as a conclusion had come from the fevered shuffling and reshuffling of images that had occupied his mind as he squelched blindly through the driving rain; but something had been achieved, something like a new solidity in his own conception of himself. He knew that he could not, now or ever, accompany Charlie to this or any barricade. He knew that, before he could look more closely at his life, there was a thing he had to do — a little thing, an insignificant thing, but to himself a thing of overriding importance. He had to finish his book; at once, without further delay. A few hours' writing, and it would be done. Nothing had ever meant so much to him.

When he had changed his wet clothes he took them through to the kitchen to hang them on the wooden frame above the stove.

'Harry!' cried Mair. 'There you are then! We were just beginning to get worried about you.'

'I only went for a walk.'

'You must have got soaked. No coat or boots or anything — are those your things? Give them to me then. I expect you'd like some tea? There's hot biscuits in the oven.'

Henry was overwhelmed. Mair fussed round him, fetching a pair of Elwyn's slippers, setting out a wonderful tea for him, wringing and hanging his clothes, stuffing his shoes with crumpled newspaper, not for a moment allowing him to move from his chair to help. As she passed him on the way out of the kitchen to fetch the shoes from his bedroom, she gave him a smile which made him long to run after her and ask *why* — why had the ice melted out of her eyes, what had he done to deserve this heaven of friendliness? But even as he framed the question, the answer came: he was now 'serious', too.

'Where's Charlie?' Henry asked, when Mair came back with his shoes.

'Poor Charlie,' said Mair, smiling. 'He's really in a state! He heard something on the wireless, on the News, but it broke down just as they were in the middle of it and he couldn't get it going again. So now he's gone off down to the village again to watch the news on Auntie Gwen's telly. Said he couldn't wait for the papers tomorrow, he was too nervous. Wouldn't wait for his tea, just got up and went.'

'Did you hear it — this bit of the News?'

'I heard the beginning, before the wireless went wrong. Something about Russia threatening to send rockets over if we tried to reoccupy that island — what is it? — the one the rebels have got control of.

But it didn't say *where* they were going to send rockets. I think it's all a lot of bluff.'

Tad, who was sitting in his chair by the fire apparently fast asleep, opened his wrinkled little eyes to remark: 'A lot of schoolboys, that's all they are. Rockets, by damn! Playing soldiers, that's all, just like El, in the boys' room, playing soldiers. He's got no brain, that boy. I tell you, Harry bach, I'd be proud to have a son like you, clever and that, but *Elwyn!* — man diawl, he can't even grow up!'

Henry and Mair exchanged secret smiles. 'Is El in the boys' room, then?' asked Henry.

'Yes. He said to tell you to go up when you'd had your tea.'

'The boys' room' was a long, shallow attic running the whole length of the house, used partly to store rubbish, partly as an indoor playground for the three boys. Here were the decorated headquarters of their various clubs ('The Ty Coch Labour League', 'The Bont Newydd Home Rule Group' and 'The Anti-Tan-yr-Allt Society' — Tan-yr-Allt was the nearest neighbouring farm), and the sad detritus of a host of passionate crazes.

Elwyn was standing near the trap-door as Henry came up the ladder. He had a number of wire hoops, of different sizes, in one hand. At his feet, covering a large part of the floor, was a map of the world. The continents and major islands had been cut, roughly, from sheets of newspaper, the principal cities and ports marked by blobs of red paint. Here and there across this map, centred usually upon one of the blobs, lay some of the wire hoops. Watkin, the eldest boy, aged ten, hovered on the other side of the map, also holding some hoops.

'Ah, Henry,' said Elwyn, 'you're back. Had a nice walk? Good. Charlie ran out of horror in the papers, so he's scuttled off to the village to see if he can find some on the telly. Watkin, what the hell do you think you're doing now?'

Watkin had taken a step forward and laid one of his large hoops, rather tentatively, in the general area of Salt Lake City. He was now regarding this move with some distrust, but obviously thought he might be able to brazen it out.

'Salt Lake City,' he said. 'Strategic Air Command, Northern Control. One-hundred-megaton bomb, altitude forty miles. That's the blast area. You've only got three more controls left now.'

'How did you get it there?'

'Long-range rocket,' said Watkin. He peered at the wild expanses of northern Russia and added hopefully: 'From Archangel. Across the North Pole.'

'Rubbish!' said Elwyn forcefully. 'That's five thousand miles. I've told you before, that's a ten-ton payload you've got there, you can't throw that lot more than fifteen hundred miles, *at the outside*. Keep to the rules, chum, keep to the rules.'

Watkin gave Henry a slightly sheepish grin, and came forward again to retrieve his hundred-megaton hoop. For a moment he hovered indecisively over the map, and then suddenly pounced, with a little yelp of intellectual triumph, to place a much smaller ring around Istanbul.

'Sub-megaton ballistic missile,' he announced with pride. 'Fired from a battleship in the Black Sea. Altitude 20,000 feet. That's only the fire area, but it's destroyed all aircraft above ground within seven miles of the fireball.'

Elwyn pondered this move and at length — Henry thought rather grudgingly — approved it. 'All right, I'll give you that. I was wondering when you'd notice Turkey tucked away down there. I'm not sure about this seven-mile destruction area from a sub-megaton missile. But I suppose you could have done the same thing with a larger rocket, fired from the ground in Bulgaria, so you'd better have it. Now you watch this, Watkin. This is going to knock you, this is really going to make you dizzy!'

Elwyn selected a medium-sized hoop and laid it down carefully in the centre of Europe. 'That's Leipzig,' he said. 'Ten megatons, altitude seven miles. You notice I haven't gone for Berlin? No point in it. I've done enough damage there with my big bomb on Stettin, right at the start. This way I really knock up your communications. Dresden's on fire. So's Chemnitz, and Magdeburg. Oh, you're in a right old mess there, Watkin! I think we can leave the rest of East Germany for the tactical boys to clean up. What do you think, Harry?'

Henry had no chance to say what he thought. Watkin was leaping and squirming around as if he desperately needed to relieve himself. 'You can't do that!' he was crying. 'You can't do that, El! Ten megatons! Where's it come from? You've got no planes left in Europe, you know that!'

'Calm down, son,' said Elwyn. 'It's all quite simple. You've been overestimating your big bangers, that's all. This lot looks very pretty, but it means damn-all.'

'This lot', which Elwyn indicated with a disdainful foot, was a newspaper silhouette of the British Isles. Five of the largest rings lay upon it, centred roughly upon London, Bristol, Liverpool, York and Edinburgh. Between them they accounted for most of the surface of England, Scotland and Wales. A smaller ring, centred on Belfast, took in the whole of Northern Ireland. Henry knelt to examine the areas of devastation more closely. He was relieved to see that the Bont Newydd district was just outside the perimeter of the Liverpool hoop.

'What do they mean,' he asked, 'these hoops?'

Elwyn knelt beside him. 'These big ones here, they're the fire area from a hundred-megaton bomb. That just means that anything inflammable, dry wood and paper and cloth, would ignite, you'd get a lot of fires starting up spontaneously and the blast winds would probably make them worse. But you wouldn't have complete destruction, and towards the edges the fires wouldn't be serious. The actual blast area's much smaller.' Elwyn laid another ring around Liverpool, encompassing an area from Chester in the south to Southport in the north. 'There, that's your real area for actual destruction, and that's where our clever lad here has made his big mistake. According to the rules, you see, we've each got ten hundred-megaton bombs — and that's all, just the ten. When the war starts, we're each allowed to set off as many as we like, simultaneously, as long as we can show that the targets are within our fire power. After that we can only have one explosion at a time, taking it in turns. Now Watkin thought he'd be clever and lay the whole of the British Isles waste with five neatly placed bombs. What he forgets is that my missile bases in England are *underground* — they can't stand up to blast, but the fire area doesn't worry them a bit. Now, I've got a missile base out here at Ipswich, and although it's within the fire area of Watkin's London bomb, it's still functioning perfectly well. That's how I was able to send that ten-megaton rocket over to Leipzig just now. Watkin thought he'd knocked all my European missile bases out, but he was wrong. It's all too easy to overestimate the power of these big ones.'

'Overestimate!' said Henry. 'Jesus!'

Rather sulkily, Watkin placed one of his smaller hoops around Ipswich. He didn't bother to give details of its size or origin. Elwyn bared his teeth in a sardonic grin. 'The bloody horse has flown now, boy,' he said.

Henry wanted very much to ask an intelligent strategic question, but he found that his heart was beating so loudly that he had to wait a moment or two in order to voice it with appropriate detachment.

'What about,' he said at last, 'these American submarines, whatjemecallits, polaris? Aren't there any of those about?'

'No, none,' said Elwyn in a lordly way. 'They make the game too easy. We agreed at the start to set off underwater nuclear devices all over the world, so that the shock waves would destroy all the submarines at one go. After all,' he added, grinning madly at his son, 'it's only a game, isn't it, Watkin?'

'Ar,' said Watkin morosely, 'but I don't reckon you play it fair, El.' He turned to Henry for support. 'He says all coastal areas under a hundred feet will be flooded, when we set these underwater bombs off. Trust him! Look at this!' He waved his hand angrily at an area north of the Black Sea. 'The whole bloody Ukraine flooded, right up to Kiev! Stalingrad flooded! Estonia, Latvia, Thingummy-onia, the whole of southern Finland, all bloody-well flooded!'

'Don't swear so much, Wat,' said Elwyn.

'Well, you do. And look at him—how much of his coastline is flooded? A miserable little bit of Norfolk and Lincolnshire and that bit round Texas, that's all.'

'And northern Italy,' said Elwyn.

'Who cares about rotten old Italy?' said Watkin, and relapsed again into his gloomy appraisal of the strategic situation.

'The trouble with Watkin,' said Elwyn to Henry, 'is that he won last time we played, when he was the Western Alliance and I was Russia, and he still thinks it was because he's cleverer than I am. But the fact is, it's very difficult for Russia to win at all. She's surrounded, and she's got a far bigger field of enemy bases to tackle. I'm not at all sure she can win, however she plays it.'

'What do you mean by "win"?' said Henry.

'Well, we reckon one of us has won when the other one has been so knocked about that he can't really do much more damage. We've only got the same number of missile sites and airfields, and we can invent where they are, as long as it's reasonable, as we go along. But, you see, his are much more concentrated than mine are, so it gets progressively more difficult for him all the time.'

'And what about people?'

'What do you mean?'

'I mean, don't you count up the probable number of people killed by each explosion? Surely that would affect who's the winner and who's the loser?'

'Certainly not!' said Elwyn scornfully. 'This war hasn't got anything to do with *people* — it's a purely military affair.'

'I see,' said Henry.

'Come on, El,' said Watkin impatiently, 'it's your turn.' He was grinning secretively now, obviously having devised a strategy which he thought would put Elwyn at a disadvantage. Henry backed slowly towards the trap-door.

'Don't go, Harry,' said Elwyn abstractedly, already concentrating on the map again.

'Must go. Sorry. Thanks. Work to do,' mumbled Henry.

When Charlie came back from the village later that evening, he brought with him, in a haversack, some cans of beer. Henry was still brooding over his typewriter when Charlie came to the door of his room.

'I've got some beer in the kitchen, Harry,' said Charlie. 'Come and join us.'

'I'll come through soon. Just got something to finish.'

'You heard about the Russians threatening to use rockets.'

'Yes, Mair told me. You must tell me all about it when I come through.'

'Don't be long then.' As Charlie was closing the door, Henry called him back.

'I say, Charlie. Has Elwyn shown you what he's got up in the boys' room? This game thing, I mean?'

'Yes. He showed me last week. It's a lot of nonsense, really, you know. It wouldn't work out like that at all, in reality.'

'What do you mean — "in reality"?'

'If it really happened. If there was a war. It would all be much quicker and more chaotic. No time for thinking — just bash, bash, bash.'

'I see.'

'Why did you ask, Harry?'

'Oh, I was just thinking. It's a funny world, Charlie.'

'It's that, all right.'

Charlie closed the door quietly, and Henry returned to his problem. The book was nearly at an end. Domenica, having failed to wean Colchester from his violent ways by argument, had at length resorted to example. At the final confrontation between Colchester and Krossov, when Krossov was at last outwitted by the English agent's brilliant manœuvres and about to meet at Colchester's hands the death which he so richly deserved, Domenica had risked her own life to come between them. Not only had she persuaded Colchester, by her courage and by her inspiration, to spare his old enemy's life, but Krossov himself, shamed by the human goodness which now shone from this beautiful woman's eyes, in one blinding flash of revelation at last saw the error of his ways. 'One human life,' cried Domenica, 'is more precious than a nation's pride' — a superb phrase, Henry thought. After a brief discussion on world politics, over which the Russian and the Englishman were astonished to find that they entirely agreed with each other, Domenica was able to convince them both that they had been the unwitting tools of wicked politicians who were leading the world to disaster in their pursuance of self-grandeur. Krossov then revealed that he had a wife and three children, none of whom he had seen for many years, in Israel; and the three ex-agents, now firm friends, set off from Aden, heavily disguised, to search the Holy Land for Mrs. Krossov, Miss Krossov, and the two Master Krossovs.

The problem facing Henry now, once the Krossov family had been reunited, was what to do with his peace-loving heroes: how to devise an ending that was at once promising, suited to their varied talents, and compatible with the idea of a future for them all, whatever might happen to the rest of the world. After poring over his little school atlas for about twenty minutes, Henry finally decided that the only spot on the globe which might not only survive a nuclear war but also be capable of supporting life was the island of Tierra del Fuego. Dredging his memory, he was unable to unearth any schoolboy memories about the flora, fauna and agriculture of this area save the useless, and indeed improbable, notion that the principal inhabitants were penguins and foxes; but this was no disadvantage. Henry was convinced that where there was soil, and a reasonably temperate climate, Colchester and Krossov would be able to devise some means for supporting the lives of the little nucleus that would ensure humanity's survival. In fact, a carefully worded advertisement in the Personal Column of *The Times* would be sure to attract those experts whose specialised knowledge would be so invaluable . . . possibly a new, peace-loving community might be brought into being even before the catastrophe occurred . . . the best minds of every country . . . it wouldn't do to get too specific . . . it was the *suggestion* that mattered.

Henry finished his book some hours later, wholly satisfied that, having done what he had to do, he had done it as well as he knew how. Stretching his aching shoulders, rubbing his eyes, he remembered his promise to Charlie and padded quietly, in stockinged feet, through to the kitchen. The house was silent, the beer cans on the table all empty. Henry looked at the alarum clock on the dresser: 2-30 a.m. — how extraordinary! It seemed no more than half an hour since Charlie had come to his door, mumbling of Russian rockets, and beer.

Henry was about to return to his own room when, poking among the beer cans to see if any were still unopened, he saw the note which had been propped up against one of them.

'The witching hour,' he read, 'and your typewriter still clacking. We're off to bed. Beer finished, sorry. I'm catching the 12-15 from Blaen tomorrow — El taking me in the Land-Rover — can you come?

'Elwyn says I'm to leave you alone now, but I must say this: when the Cossacks are watering their horses in the Conway river, and the Elwyns of the world are being tortured to make them "confess", will you remember that on the day you were asked to add your mite to oppose their might, you shut yourself away once more in your schoolboy dreams, asking only to be left "in peace"?

'Or when you see that sudden glow on the horizon, and know you have only hours to live, will you ask yourself how much your "clean" conscience is worth?

'Good night. C.'

Below Charlie's neat handwriting Elwyn had scrawled a few words: 'Sleep sound, little pig: the enemy is elsewhere.'

Chapter Eleven

'TEN to twelve,' said Elwyn. 'Time for another pint. Charlie?'

'Mixed, please. I hope this train has a corridor, man diawl. What goes in must come out.'

'Harry?'

'Bitter, please, El. Anyone got a match?'

They had been sitting in a pub near the railway station in Blaengwyrionedd for twenty minutes or more, largely in silence. Now that the facts of Charlie's departure and Henry's refusal to depart were beyond dispute, the three friends found that they had entered a conversational cul-de-sac from which they could not escape. Further discussion of what Elwyn called 'The Subject' would be futile; but the weight of those tremendous somethings that still reverberated in their minds squashed flat the little nothings that might have sustained them through the usual embarrassments of a leave-taking.

'Isn't this the pub,' said Elwyn, when he returned with the beer, 'where we used to give them a rendering of the Song of Solomon on Saturday nights, when we were all in the Sixth Form?'

Charlie grinned, his sun-burned face crinkling up, his huge ears lifting. 'I think it is, by damn!' he said, delighted. 'I'd forgotten that lark — me with a false moustache and Harry in his dark glasses — God, what a laugh!'

'Thy teeth are like a flock of sheep that are even shorn, which come up from the washing,' said Elwyn; 'whereof every one bears twins, and none is barren among them — I wish mine did!'

'Thy lips are like a thread of scarlet, and thy speech is comely,' said Charlie; 'thy temples are like a piece of pomegranate within thy locks. Harry?'

'Thy neck is like the tower of David builded for an armoury,' said Henry, 'whereon there hang a thousand bucklers, all shields of mighty men. Altogether, then, one-er, two-er——'

'Thy two breasts are like two young roes that are twins,' they cried in unison, 'which feed among the lilies. Until the day break, and the shadows flee away, I will get me to the mountain of myrrh, and to the hill of frankincense. Thou art all fair, my love; there is no spot in thee.'

They leant back in their chairs, drinking, wholly delighted with each other, and hilariously conscious of the amused, disapproving or enquiring stares they were receiving from neighbouring tables.

'Do you remember, Harry,' said Charlie, 'the night Elwyn heard he'd won a prize at the Eisteddfod, and got up on the bar at the Queen's and recited the whole of "Tintern Abbey" to the astonished public? What on earth made you choose that, El?'

'Because it is long,' said Elwyn.

Henry and Charlie roared with laughter.

Now that Elwyn had launched them on reminiscences of their schooldays the floodgates were down,

they could hardly wait for one hilarious memory to
reap its share of laughter before starting on another.
It was odd, Henry reflected, that the three of them
had been living close together for a fortnight, with
hardly a mention of the past, and that it was only
now, with barely twenty minutes left before Charlie
would have to board his train, that the tonic tide
of a shared youth should have swept over them. *Partir*,
Henry murmured to himself, *c'est toujours whatnot
un peu.*

And, sure enough, somewhere between the Public
Bar and Platform Two, laughter left them. Elwyn
stood on one foot near the barrier and rubbed the
toe of the other up and down against his calf — a
schoolboy habit which Henry recognised as a sign
that he was annoyed. 'Look here, Charlie,' he said
suddenly, as if releasing something he had intended to
hold back, 'I've been trying to keep the peace and we
can't start again now. But don't get me wrong. I
can see why you feel you've got to go, I sympathise
with you. But you're up the creek, you know that,
don't you, you're up the bloody creek. You're off
to fight the wrong enemy, mate.'

'For pity's sake, El!' said Charlie wearily. 'Must
you? Why the hell d'you have to start again now?
You've had time enough, God knows!'

'I've been thinking,' said Elwyn, morosely.

'Lord protect us. What do you want me to fight
then? The Americans?'

'If you did, you'd do as much good. Or harm. No.
Listen.' Elwyn turned to the ticket collector, who
was surreptitiously reading a tightly-folded children's

comic. 'Hey!' said Elwyn loudly into the man's ear. 'You want to be blown up?'

'What? Eh? What, what?' said the ticket collector, startled.

'I said, do you want to be blown up? Do you want to be burnt alive? Eh, eh?'

The man looked round, bewildered, half suspecting that Elwyn was a maniac with a bomb in his pocket. 'What you getting at?' he said suspiciously. Elwyn, with his lunatic grin, was certainly enough, Henry thought, to put the fear of God into anyone who didn't know him.

'Man diawl, I asked you a simple question,' said Elwyn, as if impatient at being misunderstood. 'I wondered if you were happy about it. Have you made your peace with God? Eh, eh? Have you reconciled yourself to the fact that it may be a slow death? A bit of flesh dropping off here and there, that's probably the size of it. That okay with you?'

The man smiled hopefully at Henry. 'A bit of a nut case, this one, isn'it?' he said. Then he looked over their shoulders into the empty caverns of the station, and called out: 'Now then, tickets please, all tickets *if* you please.'

Elwyn turned away, drooping a little. 'See what I mean, Charlie? That's the enemy, boy. Absolute apathy. Never thought about it. Doesn't know it's there. One of these things that's been blown up by the newspapers, nothing to do with *him*. Oh no. Arglwydd mawr, is it me that's off my nut, Charlie? Harry? I'll tell you. I went into the boys' bedroom last night, on my way to bed, and I looked at them.

I stood looking down at them. There they lay. Arms
out, blankets all over the place, chests bare. Exposed.
Abandoned. Completely vulnerable. How do they
come to sleep like that? Because they trust me. Jesus
Christ!'

Elwyn advanced on Charlie, gripped his lapel, and
pulled him towards him. 'I'm thirty,' he said grittily.
'I'm so old with worry and fear I don't give a two-
penny fuck what happens to me, I'm nearly dead
anyway. But when I look at those boys, I ask myself:
what have *you* done, Elwyn Ellis, to give them a chance
of living through a decent life? Don't ask me whether
it matters if they do or not, I'm telling you I know
in my bowels *it matters*. And what have I done? Fuck
all. Old Harry here, in his muddled way, has done
more than me. Or you. And what you're doing now
is no more than a genuflection towards the status quo,
because you're still living in the days when the form
of living mattered, because living wasn't in doubt.
But now it is, Charlie, now it is.'

Charlie's face had maintained, throughout this, a
hard rigidity which Henry had never seen before.
Stepping back now from Elwyn, straightening his
twisted coat as the guard's whistle blew, he was in
Henry's eyes a wholly different person from the one
who had been laughing over their schoolboy exploits
five minutes before.

'All right, El,' he said softly, 'I'm with you. But
Harry and I have been asked a question you haven't
been asked, and we have to find an answer. Mine's
different from his — that's a pity, but there it is. But
now it's my turn to agree with something you said —

Harry and I are not the same person. When we're laughing over what you did to Baldy in the Chemistry Lab., we're as close as we can ever be. But when it comes to a choice between Communism and death, we'll never meet. I'd rather be dead, you see. Sorry, El.'

'You'll miss your train,' said Henry.

Elwyn and Henry shook hands with Charlie in silence. The guard's whistle shrilled again. The ticket collector, bored, had gone back to his comic, and none of the three could find the appropriate last words.

'I'll write,' said Charlie.

'Do that thing,' said Elwyn.

'Best of luck, man,' said Henry.

Charlie grinned, and ran. Elwyn stood, as the train pulled out, with his arms hanging loosely and his face pulled tight in a smile which had not a trace of humour in it. Astonished, and humbled, Henry saw that tears were running down Elwyn's cheeks. Real tears.

Chapter Twelve

H ENRY spent the rest of the day wandering aimlessly around Blaengwyrionedd, alone. Elwyn
had taken the Land-Rover back to Ty Coch,
for he had work to do; Henry would catch the bus
to Bont Newydd later in the day and spend the evening
in the pub before walking up to the farm.

As if it had been waiting for Charlie's departure,
the rain, which had been drenching the district all
week, had now stopped, and the sun, astonishingly
warm, had broken through the thinning clouds to set
the pavements in the town steaming and bring the
children down to the beach to release their stored
energy in an orgy of action.

His book finished, and already receding into the
depersonalised past where all such endeavours lie,
Henry felt empty, wholly without character. He
walked the streets waiting for life to fill him with its
necessary irrelevancies, trying to uncover in himself
the lack which he felt but for which he knew no
cause. Standing by the school gates at 4-15, he
watched the tide of shouting children stream out into
the road, dodging, pushing, wheeling or riding bi-
cycles, some gay, some morose, the unused corpuscles
of the human blood-stream. Once he had belonged
among them, understood their tribal laws, walked

with sure feet through the intricate mazes of their conventions; now they passed him without a second glance, sure of his status as an outsider. They would have been amazed to learn that he knew the special words they used for the lavatories, the changing rooms, the store-cupboard under the main stairs; if he were to use these words, their natural reserve in the presence of a 'grown-up' would change to uncomfortable suspicion: he would be a spy among them. 'Sorry, sir!' cried a spindle-legged urchin, as he checked his wild run too late and cannoned off Henry's thigh. So, he was 'sir' now: one of *them*.

And yet he did not feel any older than he had when he had been running with them as of right. He knew more of the world; but the more he learned, the less he understood. It was here, under these trees near the school gates, that he had knocked Emrys Pugh, Garth Foel, to the ground after Emrys had suggested that Henry's lack of Welsh proved him to be an Englishman; and the emotion he had felt then, watching Emrys wipe the blood from his nose, was different only in degree from the emotion of that other moment, when the Cypriot boy lay dead at his feet: a surprised recognition of something in himself which could not accept the common conventions: if a man insult you, hit him; if a man resist you, kill him. Henry had not raised his fist against another since that day, and had not found himself any the worse regarded by his fellows for his eccentric refusal. Odd that it should be so much harder to resist an invitation to kill.

He walked, among a stream of children, down the long avenue towards the promenade, and the sea. In front of him walked two girls in gym-slips, their arms about each other's waists, heads together, whispering urgent secrets. They were about fifteen or sixteen — Betty Williams's age, roughly, when that commercial traveller from Norwich had seduced her on Ynys-fach after filling her with sweet cider during a lunch-time pub-crawl in his flashy little MG. After listening to Betty's tearful confession, Henry had bearded the man in his hotel, unsure himself as to what he was demanding on Betty's behalf but vaguely convinced that the man should not get away with his seduction scot-free. 'Be your age, old man. She was screaming for it.' But Henry had refused to 'be his age'; and had found himself being manœuvred out into the street, across the road, and into a churchyard; where, among looming grave-stones, he was quietly and savagely beaten up. A curious incident, apparently meaningless; and yet it had taken its place in Henry's mind as one of the familiar signposts between the principal termini of his thoughts.

On the promenade Henry sat down on a wooden bench, lit a cigarette, and stared out over the quiet sea to where the distant coastline of the Lleyn Peninsula hung mistily between sea and sky. One needs a place to call 'home', and this, for Henry, was that place. He could, he felt, sit here for ever, watching the unrepeating water play through its repertoire of moods. And yet unease would not allow him to sit for long. He had no right to sit quietly by the seashore with a peaceful mind. He had forfeited that right the day he had decided to act against his country's laws. It was not just the vague feeling that some bored police-

man might feel inspired to ask awkward questions —
although Henry, who endowed all policemen with
encyclopaedic memories and X-ray eyes, would now
have made elaborate detours to avoid passing one —
but also the even more imprecise, but firm, conviction
that he was no longer morally entitled to enjoy the
freedoms of daily life like an innocent man.

It was by now, anyway, nearly time to catch the bus
back to Bont Newydd: and somehow he felt safer,
both from the law and his own nagging conscience,
in Elwyn's village than in his own home town. Henry's
enjoyment of that bus ride across the low foothills
and up the side of the estuary towards the stone bridge
at Bont Newydd was as intense as a love affair: a
breathless catching of moments: the soft Welsh chatter
of the housewives returning from a Saturday shopping
expedition or a visit to the cinema; the clean look of
rocks and trees in the evening sunlight after the week's
rain; the greetings the bus driver gave, on his horn,
as he passed road-men or farm labourers whom he
saw on this evening trip every working day of his life;
the picking up and dropping of packages and messages
at remote corners along the route; the polite exchanges
of names between driver and passenger as they joined
or left the bus — 'Bore da, Mrs. Thomas, sut yd'a'chi
heddiw?' 'Da iawn, diolch, Mr. Williams. A chi?'
'Iawn, diolch yn fawr.' 'Good night, Mr. Williams.'
'Good night, Mrs. Parry. See you next week, then.'

It was all music in Henry's ears. He was sitting at
the front of the bus, near the door; and as the driver
pulled up outside the Gwydyr Arms in Bont Newydd
Henry turned to him, as he opened the door and

stepped down towards the road, to give his own good
night. As he did so, he saw that another passenger,
a girl, was threading her way through the shopping
baskets and bulging thighs, her head down, from a
seat at the back of the bus. There was something
familiar about her figure. In the road Henry stood
waiting, looking at the bus with love, wondering if
it could be dangerous to be seen and recognised by
some girl (Betty Williams? — not fat enough) out
of his past.

But it was not a girl out of the past he had been
thinking of. It was Bertie.

'Bertie!' said Henry, as she stepped down carefully
into the road and the door slid to behind her.

'Henry!' said Bertie.

They stood looking at each other, bemused.

'*Bertie!*' said Henry, accusingly.

Bertie hung her head a little, smiling uncertainly.
Shameless, that's you, thought Henry; and stepped
forward to pull her away from the moving bus, into
his arms; she filled the space there perfectly, and Henry
knew what it was he had been missing, that he had
not been able to put a name to.

When her little freshet of tears and incoherent
apologies had passed, Henry led her into the Gwydyr
Arms, sat her in a quiet corner, and bought rum and
Guinness for both of them. She was composed now,
smiling peacefully as she searched his face to rediscover
him.

'You didn't write,' she said, not accusingly but in
simple explanation. 'All this week. If you knew how I
watched that postman! And I said to myself, if there's

no letter on Saturday morning, I'm going to him. And there wasn't, so I came. Didn't you get my telegram?'

'I've been out all day, I'm afraid.'

'Oh, Henry — Harry — am I very wicked? Am I making it difficult for you?'

'We'll think of something,' said Henry abstractedly, feasting on her. 'Don't you worry. It's wonderful to see you.'

'Is it? Is it *really*?'

'Really and truly. I've been thinking about you all week.' This was true; for the face before him, he saw now, astonished, was the face of the new Domenica, Colchester's saviour, mother of the new world.

'But you didn't write.'

'I couldn't. Honestly, Bertie darling, you must believe me, I couldn't. I've been finishing my book and—— Oh, it's all been too ghastly.' He couldn't explain that one doesn't write letters to people who are with one, inside one, every hour of the day and night. 'Charlie's gone,' he added.

'Charlie? Oh, *Charlie*! Gone where?'

Henry explained.

'Well, I do think that's silly!' said Bertie, firmly. 'All that fuss, and then he goes creeping back, just because there's a few communists mixed up in it! Childish, I reckon. You're not,' she asked suspiciously, 'going to change your mind, too?'

Henry did some more explaining. Satisfied, Bertie beamed at him. 'I think you're wonderful,' she said. 'Isn't it extraordinary, the way some people don't seem able to think things out for themselves, the way you do? If only people would stop going around killing each other, life would be lovely, wouldn't it?' Henry grinned at her, loving her.

'Come on,' he said, 'drink up. I want to take you up the mountain, and show you off to Elwyn and Mair. Will you marry me?'

'Of course I will, silly!' said Bertie.

They left Bertie's small suitcase with the landlord of the pub, for Elwyn to collect in the morning, and set off up the path through the woods with Henry carrying a small shopping bag containing Bertie's overnight needs. They walked hand in hand, stopping to kiss from time to time. Gradually the stops became more frequent, and longer; until at last Henry had to admit that he couldn't face the prospect of sitting out the rest of the evening in Mair's kitchen, making small-talk and waiting impatiently for bedtime. Bertie was delighted. There could be little pleasure for her, at this stage, in the final act of love-making; but to know that she was needed, and to give pleasure to Henry, was at present her whole delight. Excited, and romantically stirred by the bosky setting, she followed Henry willingly up the steep banks above the path until they found a clear hollow of damp grass between the trees. When they were done, and properly dressed again, Bertie fetched stones and made a small cairn in the centre of the crushed grass.

'Wherever we make love out of doors,' she said, 'we'll leave a little pile of stones, like this. And when we're terribly terribly old, with dozens of grown-up children, we'll come back and find them, and remember.'

'You cried again, a bit,' said Henry.

'I know. But only for love.'

As they came up the path towards the point where the trees ended and the river emerged from its deep canyon, Henry took a handkerchief from his pocket and lightly bound Bertie's eyes. 'I want to give you a surprise,' he said. He led her on carefully by the hand, out into the treeless hollow below Pistyll-gwyn; then turned her to face the waterfall squarely, and unbound her eyes.

'It's almost too much, isn't it?' said Bertie, after a long awed silence. 'Nature overdoing things a bit. But — golly Moses! What a place!'

Henry moved her back a few steps to the edge of the trees. 'Stay here,' he commanded. 'Don't move an inch.'

As he walked cautiously across the mossy sward towards the river bank, Henry was thinking of Tadda and the girl he had been courting, the night he took the big fish from this very pool. He thought also of Elwyn's adventure, and looked round carefully. But the little hollow was deserted. Henry knew that it was too early in the evening for the village poachers to be out, and Owen Roberts, the bailiff, must know the same. They preferred to come out after dark, with torches, which simplified both taking the fish and escape from possible pursuers. But even if he had thought there was any danger, Henry would have been unable to resist re-creating that perfect little scene from Tadda's youth.

And there was a fish there. Not, perhaps, a large one by Tadda's standards, but Bertie wouldn't know that. As Henry knelt in the wet grass and peered down into the shallow water, he could see the dark torpedo shape lying almost motionless in the current close to the bank, no more than two feet below his face, keeping its stationary position with as little apparent effort as a man might show, lying on a bed. Henry knew the technique for taking a fish with one's hand; he had snatched baby trout often enough from the narrow streams that threaded the saltings just north of Blaen', and had listened to the boastings of boys like Elwyn, from the mountain farms, who, once the fish had entered the little hill streams in late summer, feasted on fresh salmon for weeks on end every year. The hand had to enter the water quietly, behind the fish; and then curve round, so that the fingertips could just brush the sensitive underbelly; and work slowly forwards, tickling, tickling, very gently, very slowly, hypnotising the fish with exquisite sensation until the hand was near enough to its head for that decisive grasp: fingers through gills, thumb into mouth, heave!

As soon as Henry's hand touched the water — nowhere near the fish — there was a small explosion of spray, a sinuous black flash in the stream, and the salmon was gone. Henry continued to kneel, looking down incredulously at the place where the fish had been, willing time to reverse itself a matter of ten seconds or so, and let him try again. But the fish was gone.

When he felt a tap on his shoulder, Henry stood up slowly, gazed a little vacantly at Owen Roberts, and said 'Good evening' politely. His mind, working slowly, registered first relief: for this was the explanation of the salmon's hasty departure, rather than some unknown clumsiness on his own part: good.

'Well, young sir,' said Owen Roberts pleasantly, 'we are not so lucky this week as we were last Saturday, isn'it? A fair capture, I think, sir, and I have taken the precaution of bringing the law with me this time, as you can see.'

Henry saw. Advancing towards them from one side of the hollow, more curious than alarmed, was Bertie; and from the other, a tall policeman, sternly frowning.

Oh God, police! thought Henry, in a panic; and I'm a deserter, not just a poacher. I mustn't be caught, whatever happens I mustn't be caught. Sort it out later. Now!

Henry applied the rough-house principles he had been taught in the army. Owen's hand was on his elbow; Henry pulled strongly away from the river bank, Owen pulled back even more strongly towards the river, Henry reversed the direction of his pull, and in a moment Owen was in the water.

'Run, Bertie!' cried Henry. 'Run!'

The policeman. Henry ran a few paces towards Bertie, deliberately slow; checked when the policeman, travelling fast, was nearly on him, and drove his fist firmly, but not hard, into the man's midriff. He went down with a gasp. Henry, with an encouraging cry to Bertie, ran like a stag into the trees, caught at Bertie's hand, and pulled her after him. They hid among thick brambles a hundred feet above the path, with a clear view down into the valley.

'Harry, you hit him!' whispered Bertie fiercely. 'You hit that poor policeman!'

'I know. I had to. Now shut up. I'll explain later.'

There was no pursuit. A winded policeman and a soaked bailiff could not be expected to comb the bare mountainside at this time of night for a young, strong, and quite obviously dangerous quarry. Henry didn't doubt that Owen Roberts had recognised him as a friend of Elwyn's, and he and the policeman would certainly turn up at Ty Coch the next morning to enquire about him. It was probably safe to return there now, but he would have to leave at daybreak, as soon as Elwyn had milked the cows. They could drive out on the mountain road, away from Bont Newydd; and Elwyn could say that he had not seen Henry since they had put Charlie on the train at Blaen', at noon on Saturday. It would remain a local mystery — if they were lucky.

When Owen Roberts and the policeman were out of sight and sound, on their way down the path to the village, Henry led Bertie up through the stunted oak trees to the open ridge, where a sheep-track ran along just above the tree-line towards the meeting of the two rivers above Pistyll-gwyn. She was very quiet now, and Henry sensed that she did not at all like the little incident she had witnessed, but was prepared to reserve judgment until he had told her more. So, as they plodded up beside the stream towards Ty Coch, under a glowing evening sky, he tried to justify himself. It was not easy.

'I'm a deserter, you see,' he said. 'If it was just getting caught as a poacher — well, it would have been a fair cop. And I didn't have much time to think. And then there was you.'

'Me? How do you mean?'

'I was afraid they might have taken me straight off to the police station. And I'd only just found you again, I couldn't face being parted from you so quickly.'

'You're sweet,' said Bertie; but she was reserved about it; and after a long silence she said again: 'I wish you hadn't hit that policeman so hard, though.'

'So do I,' said Henry, sincerely.

Bertie's introduction to Elwyn and Mair was overshadowed by the incident at Pistyll-gwyn. Henry saw that they liked her, and that she liked them, and was satisfied; they had heard about her, first from Charlie, later, and a little reluctantly, from Henry; and, as Elwyn said simply: 'We were hoping you'd turn up one day.' This was so obviously true that Bertie relaxed in their presence, and sat silent as Henry related the details of his escape from the law.

'Silly ass,' said Mair, smiling, a little worried.

'You must have moved fast,' said Elwyn, admiring the tactical aspects. 'People like you shouldn't break the law, Harry. It doesn't suit you.'

'I know,' said Henry, miserable.

'What now, then?' asked Elwyn. 'You can't stay here after tonight, they'll be up here, asking for you, as soon as they're out of bed. Lazy sods, these coppers — but you'd better be gone by nine, earlier if possible.'

'I know,' said Henry. 'Could you drive us out, over the mountain road, and then down to Barmouth?

We can catch the train there. You can say you haven't seen me since this morning at Blaen'. There's no reason why you should know my address in London.'

'I don't know it,' said Elwyn, truthfully.

They all thought about this in silence for a little while. Bertie, tired after her journey and all the excitement, was having difficulty in keeping her eyes open.

'Well, Harry,' said Mair at last, looking up from her sewing, 'what happens now? They're bound to come looking for you if you stay in London.'

'I shan't stay there,' said Henry quietly, his muddled mind clear for once, and decided. 'I shall go to Catterick.'

'To Catterick!' cried Elwyn.

'To the *army*?' said Bertie, awake and appalled.

'Yes. Give myself up.' Henry could not, for the moment, bear to look at Bertie. He looked at Mair. She was smiling, sphinx-like, through the eye of her needle.

'You know, don't you,' said Elwyn carefully, 'that the amnesty for deserters closes at midnight tonight?'

'I wasn't thinking of asking for an amnesty,' said Henry. 'I haven't changed my mind, or anything. I won't fight, you know that, El. Nobody can make me do that. But that business tonight, with the policeman . . . it makes me look a bit silly, somehow. There I was, fighting someone, because he threatened my freedom as a person who refuses to fight. That doesn't make sense, does it? Fighting's all the same, really. You start hitting someone, you end up by killing them. And as long as I'm a sort of outlaw, I'm in this position of having to fight my way out every time the law comes near me. It's no good, is it?'

'No, Harry,' said Elwyn. 'It's no good.'

Bertie was staring at Henry with the dazed eyes of the punch-drunk. 'They'll put you in prison,' she said, 'if you won't go for a soldier.'

'Probably. I don't know. I'm sorry, Bertie.'

Expecting more tears, Henry was astonished, and moved, when Bertie suddenly rallied to a defence he did not need.

'You're right,' she said truculently. 'I know you're right. I'm proud of you, Harry. I wish things weren't all so horrible and beastly, but I'm proud of you anyway. I shall write to you every day, and I shall wear a wedding ring, and if anyone asks me I shall say, Oh yes, well ecktewly mai husband's in prison, because he's an honest man, so there!'

Mair said quietly: 'You can stay here, if you like, Bertie. We need some help, you could easily earn your keep. You'd have to keep out of sight for a while though, until Owen Roberts forgets about Harry.'

'Please stay,' said Elwyn.

Henry looked at his friends, and at the girl he would share his life with if they were allowed to have a life, and found himself too full of love for speech.

'I used to be quite good at milking,' said Bertie, shining at them eagerly, like a child.

Postscript

7, The Cottage,
Eaton Mews South,
London, S.W.1.

Thursday.

My dear Henry,

You can imagine my joy when I read, quite by chance, the little newspaper paragraph about your case. Of course I am distressed that you will be suffering all the discomforts and humiliations of prison; but this is overshadowed by my pride that, in the last resort, you saw that you must put conscience before private loyalty. Believe me, my dear Henry, it is by such actions as yours (however insignificant they may seem in your eyes) that the idiocies of this world may one day be changed. Each private action of conscience, added to the sum of similar actions, must eventually outweigh the evil that is massed against them, and sway men's minds towards a different habit of thought.

You have not written to me, but I want you to know that, whatever may have passed between us at our last unfortunate meeting, I shall always be your friend, even if, at the moment, you cannot think of me as anything more — as in time, I hope, you may come to. My mother, Aunt Bea, Aunt Ada and Margaret

Arcadia all wish to be remembered to you with affection and admiration.

Sincerely,

Veronica.

MACLEAN & YEATMAN LTD.

Baker Street, London, W.1

Literary Agent: Authors' Representative:

13.9   AJS/MC

Dear Henry,

I was astonished to see from the papers that you've ended up in clink. I had no idea you were a pacifist. Of course I respect people who hold such views sincerely, however much I may think they are mistaken (would you, I wonder, stand by quietly while a bunch of thugs raped your sister?) but I must say you seem to have been a bit of a clot about it all. There are such things, you know, as tribunals for C.O.s and I believe they're very easy-going if they think you're sincere — put you on to hospital work, or something.

I'm afraid the occasion of this letter is a rather gloomy one. Andrew was quite *horrified* by the MS of *The Last Journey* — rang me up specially, much too early, to say so. Wanted to know if you'd gone off your chump, or something. I had to confess I hadn't read it (which set *me* down a notch in Andrew's estimation, after all the things I'd said in praise of it when I passed it along to him) and he told me what you'd done. I've now had a look at it, and I must confess I wondered if you hadn't been having a bit of a brainstorm on the quiet. Mrs. C. says it's drink, but I don't think so. I think you've gone holy, which is worse.

You just can't do it, old chap. A thriller is a thriller, and it's no good thinking you can pack a thumping great Message into something which is essentially an entertainment. I'm sending the manuscript to the address you gave me in Wales. I don't think anything could be done with this one, unless you went right through it and rewrote Domenica as the splendid character we used to know, and gave it a proper ending, with a skirmish with Krossov and all the other juicy tidbits we've come to expect from a novel by H.H.H.

Frankly, old man, I feel that I've been personally let down. If anyone has, I have made you what you are. I've rooted and grubbed for you all over London; and on top of that I have already paid you £100 (less £12-15-6 which recently came in as royalties on your last) against the advance we expected to receive for this one. But there is not going to *be* an advance on *The Last Journey*, so if I were you I'd employ my time in clink (if it's allowed) by knocking out something that has all your old, rollicking, splendid qualities, such as *The Kara-Kum Experiment*.

Things are probably a bit difficult for you now, so I won't press for repayment of what you owe immediately. But this is a business, old chum, not a public charity, and we can't let that debt stand for ever. So get writing, boy!

Yours ever,

Alex.

2357490 Hughes, H. H.,
  c/o The War Office,
   London, S.W.1.

Ty Coch,
Bont Newydd,

Tuesday. Merioneth.

Dear Harry,

You'll have to forgive a short and not very connected note.

Charlie landed at Port Gordon on 19th August, at 9 a.m. Two hours later he was killed, with three others, by a roof-top sniper, while the detachment was marching through the town. The sniper was himself killed five minutes later. Tony Cartwright (I met him that once, when he came on leave with you before Cyprus) was wounded in the shoulder. The information comes to me in a letter from him.

I know exactly how you're feeling — 'It wouldn't have happened if I'd been there.' But it would of course, if not in that way in some other. If not to him, to someone else, just as precious to others as Charlie was to us.

Oh God, the waste! And what an enigma. Charlie did what he thought was right, and because he did, all the good he was doing and would have done (to us, as well as to his Rotherhithe boys) is finished. You've done what you thought was right, and you're in gaol.

And I want to say, blast you both! Can you understand that, little pig? Damn and blast you both. Charlie said, as he left us, that you and he had been asked a question, and I hadn't. And that was true. But now it isn't. You've asked me a question. And I don't bloody well know the answer.

Come back here when they let you. If they let you out. If we live that long.

Yours ever,

Elwyn.

Ti Cock etc.

Tuesday.

Darling Harry,

Just a tiny note, in a terrible rush, to put in with Elwyn's letter. Arent I good I said a letter a day and I havent missed yet!!

Its terrible about Charly and I wont say anything because I cant — I keep on crying. Thank God it isnt you darling but its so awful anyway

Elwyn is in a dreadful state, all trembly, he spends a lot of time up in the boys room and wont even let Watkin go up. He showed me what he's got up there, this terrible map and the hoops and he was sort of hillarius as if it was funny, I was quite afraid of him. Its lucky hes got Mair.

Im still just mucking about trying to be useful and longing for you, I love you so much I dont want anything in the world at all except to have you back and safe in my arms and start a family and make a life — could we live here do you think? I'm sorry this is such an awful letter but its an awful day and Elwyn standing over me, frowning, waiting to go to the post so in grate haste darling

All my love

from Berty

PS   Mot (sheepdog) has three pups, all *beautiful*!!!

PRINTED BY PURNELL AND SONS, LTD.
PAULTON (SOMERSET) AND LONDON